The Great Gatsby

by

F. Scott Fitzgerald

Simplified,
with introduction and questions by
Celia Turvey

Longman

Longman Group UK Limited
Longman House, Burnt Mill,
Harlow, Essex CM20 2JE, England
and Associated Companies throughout the world.

© Longman Group UK Ltd 1993

Second impression 1993

Set in 10.5/13pt Linotron 300 Expert Hass
Printed in Malaysia by VVP

ISBN 0 582 08485 7

CURR
P2
.F515
GN
1993

The upper intermediate level books in the Longman Fiction series
are simplified to the 2,000 word level of the Longman Defining
Vocabulary, as researched for the *Longman Dictionary of Contemporary English*.

Contents

Introduction

"I must try to write something *new* — something extra-ordinary and beautiful and simple and intricately patterned." This is what Fitzgerald wrote to his publisher three years before *The Great Gatsby* was published in 1925. Nearly seventy years later, readers still find it new and extraordinary and beautiful, while critics and novelists are still studying those intricate, or complex, patterns.

The Great Gatsby has a special place in American literature because more than any other novel it expresses the so-called "American dream" — the belief that it is possible for anyone in America, however poor, to win success and wealth by their own efforts. But Gatsby's dream includes not only material success. It is a dream of love which only that success can buy. The book follows the course of this love from a youthful beginning to a bitter end, and it is the extraordinary nature of Gatsby's love that gives the novel its power to move our feelings and our imagination.

Scott Fitzgerald made wide use of his own life experiences in all his novels. In *The Great Gatsby* these reflects the glamour and excitement of New York life in the 1920s — a world of parties, bright lights, heavy drinking and jazz music. With the Great War behind them, Americans felt that this was a time to make money and have fun. Fitzgerald and his beautiful wife Zelda were leaders of this kind of society at that time. The Jazz Age, as Fitzgerald called it, is the setting for *The Great Gatsby*.

It was also the age of Prohibition: the law that for some years forbade the selling and drinking of alcohol. But those who wished to drink it were able to buy it illegally from men known as "bootleggers". A lot of drinking goes on in *The Great Gatsby*, which would have been more shock-ing at the time to the many Americans who supported Prohibition than it is today. However, it is interesting that the writer makes a connection between Gatsby and Daisy by making them the two characters in the book who do not drink.

Like all the main characters in *The Great Gatsby*, Fitzgerald was a midwesterner who came east. Francis Scott Key Fitzgerald was born in 1896 in St Paul, Minnesota. Unlike Gatsby he came from an old, established American family on his father's side. He began writing stories while he was still at school, and continued at college (Princeton). In 1917 the United States entered the First World War, and Fitzgerald left Princeton, without taking a degree, to join the army. Like Gatsby, he met his great love while he was in the army: the beautiful Zelda Sayre was the daughter of a judge in Alabama, where the army had sent him. They became engaged, but Zelda broke the engagement when Fitzgerald left the army and only managed to get a low-paid job in New York. To win her back he needed money and success; just like Gatsby, he gave himself up to achieving them. He did it by rewriting a novel about college life which he had begun at Princeton. *This Side of Paradise* was published in 1920 and it *was* a success. He was now able to marry Zelda. He worked hard writing short stories and another novel, to make enough money to lead the kind of life that they wanted to lead.

The Fitzgeralds moved into a house in Great Neck, Long Island, where they lived in the company of the rich and the glamorous. Great Neck and its society was the model for West Egg, in *The Great Gatsby*. The book was begun in 1922, while the Fitzgeralds were living on Long Island, but most of it was written in 1924, after they had moved to the South of France. Like many other American writers, including Hemingway, they found that it was easier, and cheaper, to live abroad. Their life on the Riviera provided the material for Fitzgerald's second most famous novel, *Tender is the Night*.

Gatsby was praised by most of the critics but did not sell at all well. Things began to go wrong for the Fitzgeralds. Money was short, they had frequent quarrels; Scott was drinking heavily; Zelda's mental health was failing. In 1930 she had a mental breakdown and for the rest of her life she was in and out of mental clinics. Fitzgerald gave way to despair. However, he moved to Hollywood in 1937 and began writing for films. He also started a novel about the film world, which was half finished when he died of a heart attack in 1940.

It was generally considered that he had not fulfilled his promise as a writer. But after his death *Gatsby*, which had seemed also to be dead, came to life again. Interest in it and in Fitzgerald grew throughout the 1940s and 50s, until *Gatsby* became part of every college literature course in the United States. The film of 1974, with Robert Redford as Gatsby, made the story known to a still wider public.

The novel is written in the first person by Nick Carraway, a young midwesterner who comes east to make a living in finance. On Long Island he becomes involved in the lives of his neighbour, Jay Gatsby, and his cousin Daisy and her husband Tom Buchanan. The main story concerns the meetings and relationships of these four people, together with Daisy's friend Jordan Baker.

The reader knows from the title that the main character of the book is Gatsby himself, but Fitzgerald does not present him to us directly: we see him only through the eyes of Nick. In fact it is not until the middle of the third chapter that Nick, and the reader, meet him at all, although by this time we have already heard some of the wild stories about him. Gatsby is a mysterious figure — he is obviously extremely rich, but no one seems to know who he is or where his wealth comes from. (At one point Tom calls him "Mr Nobody from Nowhere"). This mystery is part of his interest. Throughout the book, even in the final chapter, we are piecing together information about his background, and the sources of his wealth.

Fitzgerald gave a lot of thought to the way in which the story should be unfolded, and made changes even while it was being printed. The skill which he shows in this gives the book an added richness and depth. The main events of the story all take place within a period of three or four months, in the summer of 1922. (The passage of time is very important in the story and it is often mentioned.) These events are described by Nick, who is involved in most of them. Events where Nick is not present are told to him by other people, and retold *by* him as part of his story. This single viewpoint gives unity to the book.

Fitzgerald's skill as a writer is even more obvious in his way with words. He brings a scene to life not by describing it in detail but by *suggesting* it, with a few words that catch our imagination. The guests in Gatsby's "blue gardens", for instance, wander "among the whisperings and the champagne and the stars".

The dialogue which makes up so much of the book is wonderfully alive. We feel this is how real people talk — men of action, like Tom; stupid people, like Myrtle. Only Gatsby speaks in a careful, formal style, which Nick remarks on when he first meets him. Gatsby has chosen his manner of speaking, to fit the social position he hopes for. "Old sport", the expression he uses to address other men, suggests the fashionable English gentleman of the period. Also, because it is in the first person, Nick's storytelling often has the liveliness of someone speaking.

Nick makes a good narrator. All the other characters are basically self-centred, concerned with their own feelings and desires. Only Nick can put himself in the place of other people, and even view himself from outside. By nature he is an observer, a watcher, rather than an actor. He does have a love affair of a sort, but though this relationship with Jordan Baker runs from the first chapter to the last, it is kept in the background.

Gatsby's kind of love is on a much grander scale. Since he first kissed Daisy five years ago, his dream of her has been the driving force of his life — he has built up all his wealth in order to get her back. He seems on the point of succeeding, but he is expecting too much of Daisy. She does not have the force of character to stand by her feelings. At the end we see her as weak, selfish and cowardly — not worthy of the dream. After all, Daisy and Tom seem to belong together.

While Gatsby has built up his wealth and position from nothing, the Buchanans represent "old money". Tom is the least complex of all the main characters — a man of great physical strength which can flash into violence, unintelligent, and completely confident in himself and his own opinions. He is scornful of Gatsby from the first, and suspects the illegal nature of some of his activities. When he finally realises that Gatsby is trying to take his wife from him, he fights back and wins. The loss of Daisy is not the end to Gatsby's story. At the beginning of the book Tom's affair with Myrtle Wilson seemed to have little connection with the main story, and to be thus a sort of sub-plot. But in the later chapters we see how Myrtle and her husband bring disaster to Gatsby. It is right, though, that both Daisy and Tom are also responsible for Gatsby's fate.

Finally, the title; how are we to understand it? Could there be anything truly great about a man who built success by morally doubtful means? Or was the greatness in the reason for his actions? It is easy to imagine Tom talking about the *great* Gatsby ironically. But for Nick, despite his doubts, Gatsby was really to be admired. In the end one feels that Fitzgerald meant to leave the reader uncertain about Gatsby himself and the American dream that he represents.

1

West Egg and East Egg

Last autumn, after only six months in New York, I came back to this midwestern city where I grew up. There have been Carraways living here for seventy years: the first one was my grandfather's brother, who came here in 1851 and started the business that my father carries on today. I never saw this great-uncle, but I'm supposed to look like him.

I finished my studies at New Haven University in 1915, just a quarter of a century after my father, and a little later I went over to Europe to take part in the Great War. I liked Europe so much that I came back to the United States feeling restless. Instead of being the warm centre of the world, the Middle West now seemed like its rough edge. So I decided to go East and learn the bond business. Everybody I knew was in the bond business, so I supposed it could support one more single man. Father agreed to pay my living costs for a year, and after various delays I came East in the spring of 1922 — for ever, I thought.

I intended to find rooms in New York City, but it was the beginning of summer, and I had just left a country of green lawns and friendly trees, so when a young man at the office suggested that we take a house together in the country, it sounded like a great idea. He found a small house to rent at only eighty dollars a month. But at the last minute the firm ordered him to Washington, and I went out to the country alone. I had an old Dodge motorcar; and a Finnish woman from the village came in to make my bed and cook my breakfast. It was lonely for a few days until one morning some man, more recently arrived than I, stopped me on the road.

"How do you get to West Egg village?" he asked helplessly.

I told him. And as I walked on I was lonely no longer. I was not a newcomer any more, I was a guide, a pathfinder.

And so with the sunshine and the great bursts of leaves growing on the trees, I had the feeling that life was beginning over again with the summer.

There was so much to read, for one thing. I bought a lot of books about banking and money matters, and they stood on my shelf in red and gold, promising to unfold the shining secrets of wealth. And I had the intention of reading many other books besides. When I was at college I was interested in literature, and now I was going to bring back all such things into my life.

By chance I had rented a house in one of the strangest societies in North America. It was on Long Island, which stretches more than sixty miles east of New York. Between Long Island and the mainland lies a narrow part of the sea called Long Island Sound. On the coast, twenty miles from the city, there are two unusual formations of land, almost exactly egg-shaped. They stick out into the Sound like a pair of great eggs, separated by a small bay. But though they are so similar in shape and size they are quite different in other ways.

I lived at West Egg, the less fashionable of the two. My little house was near the sea, between two enormous houses. The one on my right was very grand by any standard. It was a copy of some French town hall, with a tower on one side, a marble swimming pool and more than forty acres of lawns and garden. I knew that a gentleman called Mr Gatsby lived there. My own house was small and ugly, but I had a view of the water, a view of part of my neighbour's lawn, and the comforting nearness of millionaires — all for eighty dollars a month.

Across the bay the white palaces of fashionable East Egg shone along the water. The history of the summer really begins on the day I drove over there to have dinner with Tom and Daisy Buchanan. Daisy was a distant cousin of mine, and

I'd known Tom in college. And some time after they were married I spent two days with them in Chicago.

Tom was one of the most powerful football players there had ever been at New Haven University. His family were extremely wealthy. Now he'd left Chicago and come East, bringing his polo ponies with him. It was hard to realise that a man of my own age was wealthy enough to do that.

I don't know why they came East. They had spent a year in France for no special reason, and then wandered here and there, wherever people played polo and were rich together. This time they were going to stay, said Daisy over the telephone, but I didn't believe it. I felt that Tom would keep moving on, as if forever searching for the excitement of some long-lost football game.

And so it happened that on a warm and windy evening I drove over to East Egg to see two friends whom I hardly knew. Their house was even grander than I had expected, a large nineteenth-century house overlooking the bay. The lawn started at the beach and ran all the way up to the front door. Along the front of the house was a line of tall windows, wide open now to the warm wind. Tom Buchanan in riding clothes was standing with his legs apart on the front porch.

He had changed since his New Haven years. Now he was a strongly-built man of thirty, with a rather hard mouth and a scornful manner. His riding clothes could not hide the great strength of that body — you could see the muscles moving when his shoulder moved under his thin coat. It was a body of great power — a cruel body.

The rough quality of his speaking voice added to the effect of bad temper which he gave. There were men at New Haven who hated him. He and I had never been close friends, but I always had the feeling that he approved of me and wanted me to like him.

We talked for a few minutes on the sunny porch.

"I've got a nice place here," he said. Turning me around by

one arm, he pointed a wide, flat hand at the lawns, the rose gardens and the motorboat tied up on the beach.

"I bought it from Demaine, the oil man." He turned me around again suddenly. "We'll go inside."

We walked through a high hallway into a bright rosy-coloured room, with long windows at each end. The windows were open and shining white against the fresh grass outside. A wind blew through the room, blowing curtains in at one end and out at the other like pale flags, and then it moved over the wine-coloured carpet, making a shadow on it as wind does on the sea.

The only completely still object in the room was an enormous sofa on which two young women were sitting. They were both in white, and their dresses were moving in the wind as if they had just been blown into the room after a short flight around the house. I stood there for a moment listening to the curtains blowing. Then Tom shut the back windows, and the curtains and the carpet and the two young women became still.

The younger of the two was a stranger to me. She was stretched full length at her end of the sofa, and she didn't move at all when I came in. If she saw me out of the corner of her eyes she gave no sign of it.

The other girl, Daisy, made an attempt to rise. Then she laughed, a charming little laugh, and I laughed too and came forward into the room.

"I'm too, too happy to see you." She laughed again, as if she had said something very funny, and held my hand for a moment, looking up into my face, as if there was no one in the world she so much wanted to see. That was a way she had. She told me in a soft voice that the name of the other girl was Baker.

Now Miss Baker's lips moved a little, and she bent her head very slightly in my direction.

My cousin began to ask me questions in her low, exciting voice. Her face was sad and lovely with bright eyes and a beautiful mouth, but it was the excitement in her voice that men found most difficult to forget.

I told her how I had stopped off in Chicago for a day on my way East, and how a dozen people there had asked me to give her their love.

"Do they miss me?" she cried happily.

"The whole town is sorrowful. All the cars have one wheel painted black as a sign of sorrow."

"How wonderful! Let's go back, Tom. Tomorrow!" Then she added to me, "You ought to see the baby."

"I'd like to."

"She's asleep. She's three years old. Haven't you ever seen her?"

"Never."

"Well. You ought to see her. She's ——"

Tom Buchanan, who had been moving restlessly about the room, stopped and placed his hand on my shoulder.

"What you doing, Nick?"

"I sell bonds."

"Who do you work for?"

I told him.

"Never heard of them," he said firmly.

This annoyed me. "You will hear of them," I answered.

At this point Miss Baker suddenly came to life, and stood up into the room. "I'm stiff," she complained. "I've been lying on that sofa for as long as I can remember."

"Don't blame me," Daisy said. "I've been trying to get you to New York all afternoon."

The butler brought in four cocktails, and offered them to us.

"No, thanks," said Miss Baker. "I'm in training."

Tom looked at her in disbelief. "You are?" He drank down his drink as if it were a drop in the bottom of the glass. "I don't understand how you ever get anything done."

I looked at Miss Baker, wondering what it was she "got done". I enjoyed looking at her. Her grey eyes looked back at me with polite interest out of a pale, charming face. I realised now that I had seen her, or a picture of her, somewhere before.

"You live in West Egg," she said. "I know somebody there."

"I don't know a single ——"

"—— You must know Gatsby."

Before I could reply that he was my neighbour, the butler came in to tell us that dinner was ready. Tom put his hand under my arm and moved me from the room.

The two young women went out before us onto a rosy-coloured porch, open towards the sunset where four candles were burning on the table. There was less wind now.

"Why *candles*?" said Daisy. She put them out with her fingers. "In two weeks it'll be the longest day in the year." She looked at us all brightly. "Do you always watch for the longest day of the year and then miss it? I always watch for the longest day of the year and then miss it."

"We ought to plan something," said Miss Baker in a tired voice, sitting down at the table as if she were getting into bed. She and Daisy talked together, in a manner that was as cool as their white dresses. They were here, and they accepted Tom and me, making only a polite effort to entertain or to be entertained. They knew that soon dinner would be over, and a little later the evening too would be over and carelessly put away. It was sharply different from the West, where an evening was hurried through its various stages.

"You make me feel uncivilised, Daisy," I admitted. "Can't you talk about crops or something?"

This remark had a strange effect on Tom.

"Civilisation is breaking down!" he burst out. "Have you read *The Rise of the Coloured Empires*?"

"Why, no," I answered, surprised.

"Well, it's a fine book, and everybody ought to read it. It says that if we don't look out the white race will be pushed under by the coloured races."

"Tom's getting very serious," said Daisy. "He reads deep books with long words in them."

"Well, these books are all scientific," said Tom. "This fellow has worked out the whole thing. Our race has produced all the things that make up civilisation — oh, science and art and all that. And if we don't watch out these other races will take control of things. Do you see?"

At this moment the telephone rang inside the house and the butler went to answer it. He came back and said something close to Tom's ear. Tom looked annoyed, and without a word he went inside.

Daisy leaned forward.

"I love to see you at my table, Nick. You remind me of a — of a rose. Doesn't he?" She turned to Miss Baker.

This was untrue. I am not even a little like a rose. She was saying the first thing that came into her head — but a warmth flowed from her, and her voice was exciting. Then suddenly she excused herself and went into the house.

Miss Baker and I looked at each other. I was about to speak when she sat up and said "Sh!" We could hear Tom talking on the telephone inside, but we couldn't hear what he was saying. Miss Baker leaned forward, trying to hear. Then the voice stopped.

"This Mr Gatsby you spoke of is my neighbour ——" I began.

"Don't talk. I want to hear what happens."

"Is something happening?" I inquired.

"You mean to say you don't know?" said Miss Baker. "I thought everybody knew."

"I don't."

"Why — Tom's got some woman in New York."

"Got some woman?" I repeated stupidly.

"Yes. She shouldn't telephone him at dinner time, though."

Almost before I had understood her meaning, Tom and Daisy were back at the table. I avoided looking at their eyes.

A few minutes later we got up from the table, and Tom and Miss Baker wandered inside. I followed Daisy to the front porch, where we sat down.

Daisy looked out into the darkening garden.

"We don't know each other very well, Nick," she said. "Even if we are cousins. You didn't come to my wedding."

"I wasn't back from the war."

"That's true." She paused. "Well, I've had a very bad time, Nick, and I'm pretty hopeless about everything."

Obviously she had reason to be. I waited, but she didn't say any more. I began rather weakly to question her about her daughter.

"I suppose she talks, and — eats, and everything."

"Oh, yes." She looked at me. "Listen, Nick: let me tell you what I said when she was born. Would you like to hear?"

"Very much."

"It'll show you how I feel about — things. Well, I asked the nurse right away if it was a boy or a girl. She told me it was a girl, and so I turned my head away and cried. 'All right,' I said, 'I'm glad it's a girl. And I hope she'll be a fool — that's the best thing a girl can be in this world, a beautiful little fool.'

"You see, I think everything's terrible anyhow," she went on. "Everybody thinks so — the most advanced people. And I *know*. I've been everywhere and seen everything and done everything."

As soon as her voice stopped I felt the basic insincerity of what she had said. It made me uneasy. I waited, and sure enough, in a moment she looked at me with a smile of satisfaction on her lovely face — she was pleased to think that she and Tom belonged to this small group of "advanced people" who knew so much about the ways of the world.

Inside, the rose-red room was full of light. Tom and Miss Baker sat at either end of the long sofa, and she read aloud to him from the *Saturday Evening Post*. When we came in she stopped reading and stood up.

"Ten o'clock," she said. "Time for this good girl to go to bed."

"Jordan's going to play in the match tomorrow," explained

Daisy, "over at Westchester."

"Oh — you're *Jordan* Baker."

I knew now why her face was familiar — she was a well-known golf player. Her face had looked out at me from many photographs of the sporting life at Hot Springs and Palm Beach. I had heard some story about her too, an unpleasant story, but I had forgotten what it was.

"Good night," she said. "Wake me at eight, won't you."

"If you'll get up."

"I will. Good night, Mr Carraway. See you soon." She went up the stairs.

"Of course you will,"said Daisy. "In fact I think I'll arrange a marriage. Come over often, Nick, and I'll sort of — oh, throw you together."

"She's a nice girl," said Tom after a moment. "They oughtn't to let her run around the country this way."

"Who oughtn't to?" inquired Daisy coldly.

"Her family."

"Her family is one aunt about a thousand years old. Besides, Nick's going to look after her, aren't you, Nick? She's going to spend lots of weekends out here this summer."

"Is she from New York?" I asked.

"From Louisville, my home town. We were girls together."

A few minutes later I got up to go home. They came to the door with me and stood side by side in a cheerful square of light. As I started my motor Daisy called: "Wait! I forgot to ask you something. We heard you were engaged to marry a girl out West."

"That's right," Tom agreed. "We heard that you were engaged."

"It's not true. I'm too poor."

"But we heard it," Daisy repeated. "We heard it from three people, so it must be true."

Of course I knew what they were talking about. The fact that people were saying I was engaged was one of the reasons I had come East. You can't stop going with an old friend because people are talking, and on the other hand I had no intention of being talked into marriage.

Their interest rather touched me. But as I drove away I felt confused about Daisy and Tom, and a little disgusted. It seemed to me that the thing for Daisy to do in this situation was to rush out of the house with her child in her arms. As for Tom, the fact that he "had some woman in New York" was really less surprising than that he had been upset by a book. He had never been concerned with the world of books and ideas, and didn't know how to deal with them.

When I reached my house in West Egg I put the car in its shelter and sat for a while in the yard. The wind had dropped, leaving a bright moonlit night. The dark shape of a moving cat wandered across the moonlight, and, turning my head to watch it, I saw that I was not alone. Twenty yards away a figure had come out from the shadow of my neighbour's house, and was standing with his hands in his pockets looking up at the stars. Something in the way he stood suggested that it was Mr Gatsby himself.

I decided to call to him. Miss Baker had mentioned him at dinner, and that would do for an introduction. But I didn't call to him, for suddenly he did something which showed he was glad to be alone — he stretched out his arms towards the dark water. I looked towards the sea myself, and could see nothing except a single green light, very small and far away, on the coast of East Egg. When I looked once more for Gatsby he had gone, and I was alone again in the darkness.

2

Mrs Wilson

About halfway between West Egg and New York the motor road joins the railroad and runs beside it a short way, to avoid an area of low ground which is being filled in with ashes. This grey land is always covered in clouds of dust, where ash-grey men are working with spades on the piles of ashes.

Above the dust you see an enormous pair of eyes, painted on a big board beside the road. Below the eyes is the name Doctor T.J. Eckleburg. The eyes of Doctor T.J. Eckleburg look out of no face, but, instead, from a pair of huge yellow glasses. I supposed that Dr Eckleburg had moved away from this unpromising area, leaving his advertisement behind him.

The train stops here, and it was because of this that I first met Tom Buchanan's mistress.

The fact that he had one was mentioned by everyone who knew him. His friends did not approve of the way he brought her with him to popular cafés, as if to show her off to the world. Though I was interested to see her, I had no desire to meet her — but I did. I went up to New York with Tom on the train one Sunday afternoon, and when we stopped by the ash piles he jumped to his feet.

"We're getting off," he insisted. "I want you to meet my girl." He took hold of my arm and forced me from the car.

We walked back along the road, under the fixed stare of Doctor Eckleburg. The only building in sight was a small block of yellow brick sitting on the edge of the waste land. One of the three shops it contained was empty; another was an all-night café, with lines of ashes leading to the door. The third was a garage — *Repairs*. GEORGE B. WILSON. *Cars bought and sold.*

I followed Tom into the garage. The inside was bare and dirty, and the only car to be seen was the dust-covered wreck of an old Ford. The owner appeared in the door of an office. He was a pale, miserable-looking man, who could have been good-looking if he were not so spiritless.

"Hello, Wilson, old man," said Tom. "How's business?"

"Not too bad," said Wilson unhappily. "When are you going to sell me that car?"

"Next week; I've got my man working on it now."

Tom was looking impatiently around the garage, and in a moment the thickish figure of a woman appeared at the office door. She was in her mid thirties, and rather fat. There was no beauty in her face or body, but a kind of animal life-force which made her strangely attractive.

She smiled slowly, and, walking through her husband as if he were a ghost, shook hands with Tom.

"Get some chairs, so somebody can sit down," she said to her husband, who hurried into the office.

"I want to see you," said Tom. "Get on the next train."

"All right."

"I'll meet you by the newspaper shop."

She moved away from him just as George Wilson came out of the office with two chairs.

We waited for her down the road and out of sight.

"Terrible place, isn't it," said Tom. "It does her good to get away. I rent an apartment in town for her where I meet her sometimes."

"Doesn't her husband mind?"

"Wilson? He thinks she goes to see her sister in New York. He's so stupid he'll believe anything."

So Tom Buchanan and his girl and I went up together to New York — or not quite together, for Mrs Wilson sat in another car.

At the newspaper shop she bought a moving-picture magazine, and in the station drugstore some face cream and some scent. Outside the station we got into a taxi and drove off.

But at once she stopped the taxi.

"I want to get one of those dogs," she said. "I want to get one for the apartment. They're nice to have — a dog."

We stopped beside an old man with a basket full of very young dogs which he was selling.

"What kind are they?" asked Mrs Wilson.

"All kinds. What kind do you want, lady?"

"I'd like to get one of those police dogs; I don't suppose you got that kind?"

The man looked doubtfully into the basket and pulled up one of the animals by the back of the neck.

"That's no police dog," said Tom.

"No, it's not exactly a police dog," said the man.

"I think it's sweet," said Mrs Wilson. "How much is it?"

"That dog?" He looked at it admiringly. "That dog will cost you ten dollars."

"Is it a boy or a girl?" she asked delicately.

"That dog? That dog's a boy."

"It's a female," said Tom firmly. "Here's your money. Go and buy ten more dogs with it."

The dog changed hands and settled down on Mrs Wilson's knee. We drove over to Fifth Avenue, where I wanted to get out, but they both insisted that I go with them.

"I'll call up my sister Catherine," said Mrs Wilson, "and Mr and Mrs McKee from the apartment below."

The apartment was on 158th Street. We went up in the elevator to the top floor, and Mrs Wilson proudly opened the door. The small living room was filled with highly decorated furniture that was much too large for it.

Mrs Wilson sent the elevator boy out to get some milk and dog food and a box for the dog. Meanwhile, Tom brought out a bottle of whisky from a locked cupboard.

Sitting on Tom's knee, Mrs Wilson telephoned her sister and the McKees, and invited them up. Then there were no cigarettes, and I went out to buy some at the drugstore on the corner. When I came back they had both disappeared, so

I sat down in the living room and waited. They came out of the bedroom just before the guests began to arrive.

I have been drunk just twice in my life, and the second time was that evening. So I don't have too clear a memory of most of the conversation. I remember that Mrs McKee had a loud, unpleasant voice, and her husband didn't say much.

The sister Catherine was an attractive girl of about thirty, who seemed to know rather more of the world than Mrs Wilson. She sat down beside me on the sofa.

"Do you live down on Long Island like Tom?" she inquired.

"I live at West Egg."

"Really? I was down there at a party about a month ago. It was given by a man named Gatsby. Do you know him?"

"I live next door to him."

"Well, they say he's a nephew or a cousin of King Wilhelm of Germany. That's where all his money comes from."

"Really?" I didn't find this easy to believe.

Catherine was looking at Tom and Mrs Wilson. "Myrtle and Tom look good together, don't they?" She leaned close to me and whispered in my ear: "You know, they both *hate* the people they're married to. They ought to get a divorce and marry each other!"

I didn't answer, but she went on: "It's really his wife that's keeping them apart. She's a Catholic, and they don't believe in divorce."

Daisy was not a Catholic, and I was a little shocked at Tom's lie.

As the evening went on the bottle of whisky — a second one — was in frequent demand by everybody, except Catherine, who "felt just as good on nothing at all". Tom sent out for some sandwiches, which were a complete supper in themselves. I wanted to get out and walk toward the park through the soft twilight, but each time I tried to go I became caught up in some wild, loud argument. Then Myrtle pulled her chair close to mine, and suddenly poured over me the story of her first meeting with Tom.

"I was on the train going up to New York to see my sister, and he was sitting facing me. He had on a nice suit and a white shirt, and I couldn't keep my eyes off him, but every time I looked at him I had to pretend to be looking at the advertisement over his head. When we came into the station he was next to me, and his body was pressing against me. So I told him I'd have to call a policeman, but he knew I didn't mean it. When I got into a taxi with him I was so excited, I kept thinking, over and over, 'You can't live forever, you can't live forever.'"

It was nine o'clock — almost immediately afterward I looked at my watch and found it was ten. The little dog was sitting on the table looking blindly through the smoke. Tom and Mrs Wilson stood face to face discussing whether Mrs Wilson had any right to mention Daisy's name.

"Daisy! Daisy! Daisy!" shouted Mrs Wilson. "I'll say it whenever I want to! Daisy! Dai ——"

Making a short, sharp movement, Tom broke her nose with his open hand.

There was blood and confusion everywhere. While Catherine and Mrs McKee were comforting Myrtle and shouting at Tom, Mr McKee and I slipped out of the room and away.

3

Meeting Mr Gatsby

There was music from my neighbour's house through the summer nights. In his blue gardens men and girls came and went, floating among the whisperings and the champagne and the stars. In the afternoon by the shore I watched his guests swimming in the Sound, or lying in the sun on the hot sand, or water-skiing from his two motorboats.

At weekends his big open car became a bus, carrying groups of people to and from the city between nine in the morning and long past midnight, while his second car met all the trains at the station. And on Mondays eight servants, including an extra gardener, worked all day to repair the damage from the night before. Every Friday five boxes of oranges and lemons arrived from a fruit shop in New York — every Monday these same oranges and lemons left his back door in a pile of empty halves.

About once in two weeks there was a really big party. The trees were all covered in coloured lights and a dance floor was laid down on the lawn; a big group of musicians came down from New York to play music for dancing. Wonderful food arrived, with dozens of waiters to serve it, and in the main hall a bar was set up, serving every possible kind of alcoholic drink. I remember the sense of excitement at the beginning of the party.

By seven o'clock the last swimmers have come in from the beach and are dressing upstairs; cars from New York are drawing up every minute, and already the halls and sitting rooms are full of girls in bright dresses with the newest, strangest hairstyles. Trays of cocktails are floating through the garden outside, until the air is alive with talk and laughter.

The lights grow brighter as darkness falls, and now the musicians are playing cocktail music and the voices are higher and louder. Laughter is easier minute by minute. The party has begun.

I believe that on the first night I went to Gatsby's house I was one of the few guests who had actually received an invitation. People were not invited — they went there. They got into cars which carried them out to Long Island, and somehow they ended up at Gatsby's door. Once they were there they were introduced to Gatsby by someone who knew him. Sometimes they came and went without having met Gatsby at all.

I had been actually invited. A chauffeur in a pale blue uniform crossed my lawn early that Saturday morning with a surprisingly formal note from his employer: the honour would be entirely Gatsby's, it said, if I would attend his "little party" that night. He had seen me several times, and had intended to call on me, but something had always prevented it — signed Jay Gatsby.

I went over to his lawn a little after seven, and wandered around, rather uneasy among all these people I didn't know. As soon as I arrived I tried to find my host, by asking various guests where he was. But they stared at me in such a surprised way that I gave up and made my way to the cocktail table — the only place in the garden where a single man could stand about without looking odd.

I was still there some time later, when Jordan Baker came out of the house and stood at the top of the steps looking down into the garden.

"Hello!" I shouted, advancing towards her.

"I thought you might be here," she answered, as I came up. "I remembered you lived next door to —"

She was interrupted by two girls in yellow dresses, who stopped at the foot of the steps.

"Hello!" they cried together. "Sorry you didn't win."

That was for the golf competition. She had lost in the last

match the week before.

"You don't know who we are," said one of the girls in yellow, "but we met you here about a month ago."

"You've changed the colour of your hair since then," remarked Jordan.

With Jordan's slim golden arm resting in mine, we went down the steps and wandered about the garden. A tray of cocktails floated at us through the twilight, and we sat down at a table with the two girls in yellow and three men.

"I like to come to these parties," said one of the girls. "I never care what I do, so I always have a good time. When I was here last I tore my dress on a chair, and he asked me my name and address — a week later I got a parcel with a beautiful new evening dress in it. Two hundred and sixty-five dollars."

"Did you keep it?" asked Jordan.

"Sure I did. I was going to wear it tonight, but it was too big in the top, and had to be made smaller."

"There's something funny about a fellow that'll do a thing like that," said the other girl. "He doesn't want any trouble with anybody."

"Who doesn't?" I inquired.

"Gatsby. Somebody told me —"

The two girls and Jordan leaned together.

"Somebody told me they thought he killed a man once."

A current of excitement passed through all of us.

"Now I heard," said one of the men, "that he was a German spy during the war."

"Oh no," said the girl, "he was in the American army."

It seemed that Gatsby was a man whom everybody whispered about.

Supper was now being served, and Jordan invited me to join her group of friends, who were spread around a table on the other side of the garden. They were quiet, respectable people from East Egg, who seemed not to want to mix with the rest of the guests.

After half an hour Jordan whispered to me, "Let's get out.

This is much too polite for me."

We got up, and she explained that we were going to find the host, because I had never met him.

The bar, where we looked first, was crowded, but Gatsby was not there. She couldn't find him from the top of the steps, and he wasn't on the porch. Then we tried an important-looking door, and walked into a great library.

A fat, middle-aged man with large round glasses was sitting on the edge of a great table, staring unsteadily at the shelves of books. He looked drunk. As we entered he turned and looked at us excitedly.

"What do you think?" he demanded.

"About what?"

He waved his hands towards the bookshelves.

"About the books. I thought they were just for show — but they're *real*! They have pages and everything. Look! Let me show you." He pulled down a heavy, serious-looking book and opened it.

"Who brought you?" he demanded. "I was brought by a woman I met somewhere last night. I've been drunk for about a week now, and I thought it might make me better to sit in a library."

"Has it?"

"I can't tell yet. I've only been here an hour. Did I tell you about the books? They're real. They're ——"

"You told us." We went back outside.

There was dancing now in the garden, and the pairs of dancers moved in circles round the dance floor. A famous singer sang a song, some actors acted a funny scene, and champagne was served in glasses bigger than finger-bowls. By midnight the fun was louder and wilder. From all over the garden happy, empty bursts of laughter rose toward the summer sky.

I was still with Jordan Baker. We were sitting at a table with a man of about my age and a girl who laughed all the time. I was enjoying myself now. I had taken two glasses of champagne, and the scene had changed before my eyes into something deep and meaningful.

The man looked at me and smiled.

"Your face is familiar," he said politely. "Weren't you in the army during the war? Perhaps we were in the same unit — were you in the First Division?"

"Why, yes."

We talked for a moment about some wet, grey little villages in France. Obviously he lived in this neighbourhood, for he told me that he had just bought a sea-plane, and was going to try it out in the morning.

"Want to go with me, old sport? Just near the shore along the Sound."

I accepted. I was just going to ask his name when Jordan looked around and smiled. "Having a good time now?"

"Much better." I turned again to my new friend. "This is an unusual party for me. I haven't even seen the host. I live over there —" I waved a hand in the direction of my house, "and this man Gatsby sent over his chauffeur with an invitation."

For a moment he looked at me as if he didn't understand.

"I'm Gatsby," he said suddenly.

"What!" I cried. "Oh, I'm so sorry."

"I thought you knew, old sport. I'm afraid I'm not a very good host."

He smiled understandingly. It was one of those rare smiles with a quality of comfort in it, that you may come across four or five times in life. It seemed to face the whole world for a moment, and then fixed on *you*. It understood you as you wanted to be understood, and believed in you as you would like to believe in yourself. Then the smile disappeared, and I was looking at a fashionably dressed young man, a year or two over thirty, whose formal way of speaking was very nearly funny. Some time before he introduced himself I'd got a strong feeling that he was picking his words with care.

At this moment a butler hurried towards him with the information that Chicago was calling him on the telephone.

"Excuse me. I will rejoin you later," he said politely.

When he was gone I turned to Jordan, to tell her of my surprise. I had expected Gatsby to be quite different — older, fatter, red-faced.

"Who is he?" I demanded. "Do you know?"

"He's just a man named Gatsby."

"Where is he from, I mean? And what does he do?"

"Now *you*'ve started on the subject," she said with a pale smile. "Well, he told me once he had been to Oxford University. However, I don't believe it."

"Why not?"

"I don't know. I just don't think he went there."

There was really something very mysterious about Gatsby's background. Surely young men didn't just appear out of nowhere and buy a grand house on Long Island Sound?

The band began to play some loud music. At this moment my eye fell on Gatsby, standing alone on the steps and looking from one group to another with approving eyes. His skin was smooth and browned by the sun, and his short hair looked as if it was cut every day. I could see nothing mysterious about him. I wondered if the fact that he was not drinking helped to mark him off from his guests, for it seemed that he grew more correct as everyone else grew wilder. People were singing loudly, girls were falling backward playfully into men's arms, but no one fell backward on Gatsby.

Gatsby's butler was suddenly standing beside us.

"Miss Baker?" he inquired. "Excuse me, but Mr Gatsby would like to speak to you alone."

Jordan gave me a look of extreme surprise and followed the butler toward the house. I noticed that she wore her evening dress, all her dresses, like sports clothes.

An hour later I decided that it was time to go home. As I waited for my hat in the hall the door of the library opened and Jordan and Gatsby came out together. He was speaking eagerly to her, until some other guests came up to say goodbye.

Jordan's friends were calling to her from the porch, but she came over to me. "I've just heard the strangest thing," she whispered. "How long were we in there?"

"Why, about an hour."

"It was . . . so strange. But I promised I wouldn't tell it. Please come and see me . . . telephone book . . . under the name of Mrs Sigourney Howard . . . my aunt . . ." She was hurrying off as she talked.

The last of Gatsby's guests were gathered around him. I felt rather guilty that on my first appearance I had stayed so late, and tried to explain that I'd hunted for him early in the evening.

"Don't mention it," he said eagerly. "And don't forget we're going up in the sea-plane tomorrow morning, at nine."

Then the butler, behind his shoulder:

"Philadelphia wants you on the phone, sir."

"All right, I'll be there in a minute . . . Good night, old sport . . . Good night." He smiled, and suddenly it seemed right to be among the last to leave, as if he had wanted it all the time.

Reading over what I have written so far, I see I have given the idea that the events of three evenings were all that interested me. But in fact, at the time they were just some events among others in a crowded summer — they did not seem specially important to me until much later.

Most of the time I worked. My days usually followed the same pattern: I arrived at my place of work in the early morning, and stayed there until the evening. I was friendly with the other clerks and lunched with them in dark, crowded restaurants. I took dinner usually at the Yale Club, and then I went to the library and studied money matters for an hour. After that I walked down Madison Avenue and over 33rd Street to the station, to catch my train back to West Egg.

For a while I lost sight of Jordan Baker, and then in the middle of the summer I found her again. At first I was proud to go places with her, because she was a famous golf player, and everyone knew her name. Then it was something more. I wasn't in love, but I felt a sort of tender wish to understand her. The cold, scornful face that she turned to the world hid something — and one day I found what it was.

When we were at a house-party together up in Warwick, she left a borrowed car out in the rain with the top down, and then lied about it. Suddenly I remembered the story about her that I'd tried to think of that night at Daisy's. At her first big golf match there was a scandal that nearly reached the newspapers — a suggestion that she had moved her ball from a bad place in order to win.

Jordan Baker was dishonest. She couldn't bear to be at a disadvantage, so she used deceit to get what she wanted. In this way she was able to keep that cool, proud smile turned to the world. I realised that she avoided clever men. She felt safer with people who would not doubt her standards of behaviour.

It made no difference to me. Dishonesty in a woman is a thing you never blame deeply — I was sorry, and then I forgot. It was on that same house-party that we had a strange conversation about driving a car. It started because she drove too close to some workmen on the road.

"You ought to drive more carefully," I told her.

"I am careful."

"No, you're not."

"Well, other people are. They'll keep out of my way."

"Suppose you met somebody just as careless as yourself."

"I hope I never will," she answered. "I hate careless people. That's why I like you."

Her grey eyes stared straight ahead, but she had made a change in our relationship, and for a moment I thought I loved her. But I am full of rules that stop me from doing what I want to do. I knew that before I was free I had to break off that understanding with the girl back home, to whom I had been writing letters once a week.

You see, I am one of the few honest people that I have ever known.

4

Gatsby and Daisy

One morning late in July, Gatsby's splendid car pulled up outside my door. It was the first time he had visited me, though I had attended two of his parties, gone up in his sea-plane and made frequent use of his beach.

"Good morning, old sport. You're having lunch with me today and I thought we'd drive up to town together."

He saw me looking with admiration at his car.

"It's pretty, isn't it? Haven't you ever seen it before?"

I'd seen it. Everybody had seen it. It was enormous; a rich creamy yellow, with green leather seats. We set off.

I had talked with him a number of times in the past month and found, to my disappointment, that he had little to say. I had felt at first that he was someone who mattered, but now this feeling had disappeared: he had become simply the owner of a splendid house next door.

And then came that surprising ride. As we talked, Gatsby seemed strangely uncertain of himself, and began leaving his sentences unfinished. "Look here, old sport," he broke out, "what's your opinion of me, anyhow?"

I began making the kind of general remarks which that question deserves.

"Well, I'm going to tell you something about my life," he interrupted. "I don't want you to get a wrong idea of me from all these stories you hear. I'll tell you God's truth.

"I am the son of some wealthy people in the Middle West — all dead now. I was brought up in America, but educated at Oxford University, in England, because the men in my family were always educated at Oxford."

He looked at me sideways — and I knew why Jordan Baker

had believed he was lying. He hurried the phrase
at Oxford", or swallowed it, as if it troubled him.

"My family all died and I inherited a good dea
After that I lived like a lord in all the capitals of Europe —
Paris, Venice, Rome — collecting jewels, hunting wild animals,
painting a little, and trying to forget something very sad that
happened to me long ago."

With an effort I managed to hold back my laughter. I didn't
believe a word of it.

"Then came the war, old sport. I was glad, and I tried very
hard to die, but some magic seemed to keep me alive. I was
made an officer when the war began, and put in charge of a
machine-gun unit. In the Argonne Forest I took my men far
in front of the foot soldiers. We stayed there two days and
two nights, a hundred and thirty men with sixteen guns, and
when the foot soldiers came up at last they found the flags
of three German divisions among the piles of dead. I was given
a higher rank, and every government on our side gave me
a decoration — even Montenegro, little Montenegro down on
the Adriatic Sea!"

He reached into his pocket, and pulled out a circle of metal
on a coloured band.

"That's the one from Montenegro."

To my astonishment, the thing looked real. "Major Jay
Gatsby," I read, "For Courage Extraordinary."

"Here's another thing I always carry. A memory of Oxford
days. It was taken in Trinity College."

It was a photograph of six or seven young men standing
under an arch, with towers behind them. There was Gatsby,
looking a little, not much, younger.

Then it was all true. I imagined him in his palace in Venice,
with tiger skins on the walls, staring into a chest of rich, dark
jewels to ease the pain of his broken heart.

"I'm going to ask you to do a big thing for me today," he
said, "so I thought you ought to know something about me. I
didn't want you to think I was just some nobody." He hesitated.

"You'll hear about it this afternoon."

"At lunch?"

"No, this afternoon. I happened to find out that you're taking Miss Baker to tea."

"Do you mean you're in love with Miss Baker?"

"No, old sport, I'm not. But Miss Baker has kindly agreed to speak to you about this matter."

I hadn't the faintest idea what "this matter" was, but I was more annoyed than interested. I hadn't asked Jordan to tea in order to discuss Mr Jay Gatsby.

He wouldn't say another word. We drove on, beside the valley of ashes. At Wilson's garage I caught sight of Mrs Wilson working the pump with her usual animal energy.

Gatsby was driving very fast.

I heard the sound of a motorcycle, and a policeman rode up beside us. Gatsby stopped. Taking a white card from his pocket, he waved it before the man's eyes.

"Right you are!" agreed the policeman, raising his cap. "Know you next time, Mr Gatsby. Excuse *me!*"

"What was that?" I inquired. "The picture of Oxford?"

"I was able to do the Chief of Police a favour once, and he sends me a Christmas card every year."

I met Gatsby for lunch in a little restaurant on Forty-Second Street. There was someone with him: a small, middle-aged man with a flat nose and tiny eyes.

"Mr Carraway, this is my friend Mr Wolfshiem."

We sat down at our table and ordered our food.

"This is a nice restaurant," said Mr Wolfshiem. "But I like the old Metropole better, across the street."

"It's too hot over there," said Gatsby.

"Hot and small — but full of memories. Filled with faces dead and gone. I'll never forget the night they shot Rosy Rosenthal there. There were six of us at the table, and Rosy had been eating and drinking all evening. At four o'clock in the morning the waiter came up to him with a funny look and said somebody wanted to speak to him outside. I told him not to go."

"Did he go?" I asked.

"Sure he went. He turned around in the door and said to us 'Don't let that waiter take away my coffee!' Then he went out into the street, and they shot him three times in his full stomach and drove away."

He looked at me and said suddenly: "I understand you're looking for a business connection."

Gatsby answered for me. "Oh, no, Meyer, this isn't the man! We'll talk about that some other time."

We had nearly finished our meal when Gatsby looked at his watch, jumped up and hurried from the room.

"He has to telephone," said Mr Wolfshiem. "A business matter. Fine fellow, isn't he. A perfect gentleman. He went to Oxford College in England."

"Have you known Gatsby for a long time?" I inquired.

"Some years. I met him just after the war, and we've done a lot of business — I've helped him and he's helped me."

When Gatsby returned, Mr Wolfshiem took his leave.

"I'll leave you two young men to discuss your sports and your young ladies," he said. We shook hands.

"Meyer Wolfshiem's quite a character around Broadway," said Gatsby after he had gone.

"Who is he?" I asked. "How did he make his money?"

"Oh, in various ways." Gatsby hesitated. "Do you remember that big baseball scandal, back in 1919? Well, Meyer was responsible for that. He made a lot of money out of it."

I was astonished. "Why isn't he in prison?"

"They can't get him, old sport. He's a clever man."

I insisted on paying the check. As the waiter brought my change I noticed Tom Buchanan across the crowded room.

"Come along with me for a minute," I said to Gatsby. "I've got to say hello to someone."

When he saw us Tom jumped up eagerly. "Where've you been? Daisy's furious because you haven't telephoned."

"This is Mr Gatsby, Mr Buchanan."

They shook hands, and an unusual troubled look came over Gatsby's face.

"How've you been, anyhow?" demanded Tom of me. "How'd you happen to come up this far to eat?"

"I've been having lunch with Mr Gatsby."

I turned towards Mr Gatsby, but he was no longer there.

That afternoon, in the tea garden at the Plaza Hotel, Jordan Baker told me this story. The place was Louisville, the small midwest town where she grew up; the time was the year the United States entered the Great War.

One October day in 1917 — (said Jordan) — I was walking along the street where Daisy Fay lived. She was just eighteen, two years older than me, and by far the most popular of all the young girls in Louisville. I admired her a lot. She dressed in white, and had a little white car, and all day long the telephone rang in her house and excited young officers demanded to take her out that night.

When I came opposite her house that morning her car was in the road, and she was sitting in it with an officer I had never seen before. They were so interested in each other that she didn't see me until I was quite near.

"Hello, Jordan," she called. "Please come here."

She asked if I was going to the Red Cross to sew things for the soldiers. I was. Well then, she said, would I tell them that she couldn't come that day? While she was speaking, the officer looked at Daisy in a way that every young girl wants to be looked at sometime. His name was Jay Gatsby, and I didn't lay eyes on him again for over four years — even after I'd met him on Long Island I didn't realise it was the same man.

That was 1917. By the next year I had a few young men myself, and I began to play in golf competitions, so I didn't see Daisy very often. She went with a slightly older crowd — when she went with anyone at all. There was a

story going around that her mother had found her pack-
ing her bag one night to go to New York and say goodbye
to a soldier who was going overseas. They stopped her, of
course.

By the next autumn she was happy again, happy as ever,
and in February she was said to be promised in marriage
to a man from New Orleans. In June she married Tom
Buchanan of Chicago, with more splendid ceremony than
Louisville ever knew before. He came down with a hundred
people in four private cars, and hired a whole floor of the
hotel, and the day before the wedding he gave her a string
of pearls valued at three hundred and fifty thousand
dollars.

I was an attendant at her wedding. The evening before, I
came into her room half an hour before the grand dinner,
and found her lying on her bed as lovely as the June night in
her flowered dress — and as drunk as a monkey. She had a
bottle of wine in one hand and a letter in the other.

"Never had a drink before," she said.

"What's the matter, Daisy?"

I was frightened: I'd never seen a girl like that before.

"Here, dearest." She put her hand in a wastebasket and
pulled out the string of pearls. "Take them downstairs and
give 'em back to whoever they belong to. Tell 'em all Daisy's
changed her mind. Say: 'Daisy's changed her mind!'"

She began to cry — she cried and cried. I rushed out and
found her mother's maid, and we locked the door and got
her into a cold bath. She wouldn't let go of the letter. She took
it into the bath with her, until it was a wet ball.

But she didn't say any more. We put ice on her forehead and
got her back into her dress, and half an hour later the pearls
were around her neck and she went down to dinner.

Next day at five o'clock she married Tom Buchanan, and
started off on a three months' trip to the South Seas.

I saw them in Santa Barbara when they came back, and
I thought I'd never seen a girl so mad about her husband. If

he left the room for a minute she'd say: "Where's Tom gone?" and look uneasy until he came back again. She used to sit on the sand with his head on her knee, rubbing her fingers over his eyes and looking at him with deepest delight. That was August. A week after I left Santa Barbara Tom had a car accident, which was reported in the newspapers. There was a girl with him, whose arm was broken — she was one of the maids in the Santa Barbara hotel. That was the first of Tom's affairs with other girls.

The next April Daisy had her child, and they went to France for a year or two. Then they came back to Chicago to settle down. They moved with a fast crowd, all of them young and rich and wild, but Daisy came out untouched by any scandal. Perhaps because she doesn't drink. It's a great advantage not to drink among hard-drinking people.

Well, about six weeks ago, she heard the name Gatsby for the first time in years. It was when I asked you — do you remember? — if you knew Gatsby in West Egg. After you had gone home she came into my room and woke me up, and said: "What Gatsby?" and when I described him, she said in the strangest voice that it must be the man she used to know. It wasn't until then that I connected this Gatsby with the officer in her white car.

When Jordan had finished telling all this we had left the Plaza and were driving in a carriage through Central Park.

"It was a strange chance that brought him so near her," I said.

"But it wasn't a chance at all."

"Why not?"

"Gatsby bought that house so that Daisy would be just across the bay."

I remembered my first sight of Gatsby, staring out across the bay — it had not been the stars, then, which seemed to fill him with such feeling. Now he came alive to me.

"He wants to know," said Jordan, "if you'll invite Daisy to

your house some afternoon and then let him come over."

I was astonished that he should demand so little. He had waited five years and bought a great house — so that he could "come over" some afternoon to a stranger's garden.

"Why didn't he ask you to arrange a meeting?"

"He wants her to see his house," she explained. "I think he half expected her to wander into one of his parties, but she never did. Then he began asking people if they knew her, and I was the first one he found."

"Does Daisy want to see Gatsby?" I asked.

"She mustn't know. You just have to invite her to tea."

It was dark now, and I put my arm around Jordan's golden shoulder and drew her towards me and asked her to dinner.

Suddenly I wasn't thinking of Daisy and Gatsby any more. I tightened my arms around her. Her pale, scornful mouth smiled, and so I drew her up closer, this time to my face.

5

The Tea-party

When I came home to West Egg at two in the morning, light was shining all over my garden. Turning a corner, I saw that it came from Gatsby's house, lit from top to bottom. At first I thought it was another party, but there wasn't a sound. As my taxi drove noisily away I saw Gatsby walking towards me across his lawn.

"Your place looks like an entertainment hall," I said.

He turned his eyes towards it. "I have been looking into some of the rooms. Suppose we have a bathe in the swimming pool, old sport? I haven't used it all summer."

"It's too late. I've got to go to bed."

"All right." He waited, looking at me eagerly.

"I talked with Miss Baker," I said after a moment. "I'm going to call up Daisy tomorrow and invite her over here to tea."

"Oh, that's all right," he said carelessly. "I don't want to put you to any trouble."

"What day would suit you?"

"What day would suit *you*?" he corrected me quickly. "How about the day after tomorrow, at four o'clock?"

He thought for a moment. "I want to get the grass cut."

We both looked down at the grass — there was a sharp line where my untidy lawn ended and his well-kept one began. I suspected that he meant my grass.

"There's another little thing." He hesitated. "I thought — look here, old sport, you don't make much money, do you?"

"Not very much."

"I thought you didn't, if you'll pardon my — you see, I carry on a little business on the side, a sort of side line, you understand. And I thought that if you don't make very much — you're selling bonds, aren't you, old sport?"

"Trying to."

"Well, this would interest you. It wouldn't take up much of your time and you might pick up a nice bit of money."

In a different situation, that conversation might have changed my life. But I realised that his offer was made to repay me for the service I was about to perform for him — so how could I accept it?

"I've got my hands full," I said. "Thanks, but I couldn't take on any more work."

I called up Daisy from the office next morning, and invited her to come to tea. "Don't bring Tom," I told her.

On the day agreed upon it was raining heavily. At eleven o'clock a man in a raincoat knocked at my door and said Mr Gatsby had sent him over to cut my grass. I remembered I had to go into the village to buy some cups and lemons and flowers, and to ask my Finnish woman to come back.

The flowers were unnecessary, for at two o'clock a great

mass of flowers arrived from Gatsby's, with numerous pots to hold them. An hour later the front door was opened nervously, and Gatsby, in a white suit, silver shirt, and gold-coloured tie, hurried in. He was pale, and there were dark signs of sleeplessness beneath his eyes.

"Is everything all right?" he asked at once.

"The grass looks fine, if that's what you mean."

"What grass?" he inquired. "Oh, the grass in the yard." He looked out of the window at it, but I don't believe he saw a thing. "Have you got everything you need in the way of — of tea?"

I took him into the kitchen. Together we examined the twelve lemon cakes from the village shop.

"Will they do?" I asked.

"Of course, of course! They're fine!"

He sat down in the living room, and began turning the pages of one of my books. From time to time he looked miserably towards the window. Finally he got up and informed me, in an uncertain voice, that he was going home.

"Why's that?"

"Nobody's coming to tea. It's too late!"

"Don't be silly; it's just two minutes to four."

At that moment there was the sound of a car turning into my drive. I went out into the yard and saw a large car coming up the drive. The chauffeur stopped, and Daisy's face looked out at me with a delighted smile.

"Is this really where you live, my dearest one?"

Her musical voice was as exciting as ever. "Are you in love with me," she said low in my ear, "or why did I have to come alone?"

"That's a secret. Tell your chauffeur to go far away and spend an hour."

We went in. To my great surprise, the living room was empty.

Then we heard a light knocking at the front door. I went and opened it. Gatsby, pale as death, was standing staring miserably into my eyes. He marched by me into the hall and disappeared into the living room.

For half a minute there wasn't a sound. I could feel my own heart beating loudly. Then I heard Daisy's clear voice.

"I certainly am very glad to see you again."

I had nothing to do in the hall, so I went into the room.

Gatsby was leaning stiffly against the fireplace and Daisy was sitting on the edge of a hard chair. Neither of them was speaking.

"We've met before," said Gatsby now, in a low voice.

"We haven't met for many years," said Daisy flatly.

"Five years next November," said Gatsby at once, and there was another silence.

Then my Finnish woman brought in the tea, and we were able to occupy ourselves by passing round cups and cakes. Daisy and I began to talk, and Gatsby looked from one to the other of us with unhappy eyes. After a little while I made an excuse and got to my feet.

"Where are you going?" demanded Gatsby anxiously.

"I'll be back."

"I've got to speak to you about something before you go." He followed me wildly into the kitchen, closed the door, and whispered "Oh God!" in a miserable way.

"What's the matter?"

"This is a terrible mistake," he said, shaking his head from side to side. "A terrible, terrible mistake."

"You're just embarrassed, that's all," and luckily I added: "Daisy's embarrassed too."

"She's embarrassed?" he repeated unbelievingly.

"Just as much as you are."

"Don't talk so loud."

"You're acting like a little boy," I broke out. "Not only that, but you're rude. Daisy's sitting in there all alone."

He raised his hand to stop my painful words, gave me a despairing look, and went back into the other room.

I walked out the back way, just as Gatsby had done earlier. It was raining hard again, and I ran to a huge black tree,

whose thick leaves gave some shelter. There was nothing to
look at from under the tree except Gatsby's enormous house,
so I stared at it for half an hour.

Then the sun shone again, and I felt it was time to go back.
I went in — after making every possible noise in the kitchen
— but I don't believe they heard a sound. They were sitting at
either end of the sofa, looking at each other, and all embarrassment was gone. Daisy's face was marked with tears, and
when I came in she began rubbing it with her handker-
chief before a mirror. But there was a change in Gatsby that
was simply astonishing — his joy shone from him and filled
the little room.

"Oh, hello old sport," he said, as if he hadn't seen me for
years.

"It's stopped raining."

"Has it?" When he realised what I was talking about he
smiled happily and repeated the news to Daisy. "What do you
think of that? It's stopped raining."

"I'm glad, Jay."

"I want you and Daisy to come over to my house," he said.
"I'd like to show her around."

Daisy went upstairs to wash her face, while Gatsby and I
waited on the lawn.

"My house looks good, doesn't it?" he demanded. "See how
the whole front of it catches the light."

I agreed that it was splendid.

His eyes went over it, every arched door and square tower.

"It took me just three years to earn the money that bought it."

"I thought you inherited your money from your father."

"I did, old sport, but I lost most of it during the war."

I think he hardly knew what he was saying, for when I
asked him what business he was in he answered: "That's my
affair", before he realised that it was an unsuitable reply.

"Oh, I've been in several things," he corrected himself. "I
was in the drugstore business and then I was in the oil business.
But I'm not in either one now."

Just then Daisy came out of the house.

"That huge place *there*?" she cried, pointing.

"Do you like it?"

"I love it, but I don't see how you live there all alone."

"I keep it always full of interesting people, night and day. People who do interesting things. Famous people."

Instead of cutting across the lawn we went down the road and entered by the main gate. Daisy admired the view of the house standing dark against the sky, she admired the gardens, rich with sweet-smelling flowers.

It was strange to reach the marble steps and find no movement of bright dresses in and out of the door, and to hear no sound but bird voices in the trees. And inside, as we wandered through the great rooms, I felt that there were guests hidden behind every sofa and table, under orders to be silent until we had passed through.

We went upstairs, through old-style bedrooms full of fresh flowers, through dressing rooms and bathrooms with baths sunk in the floor. We went into one room where a young man was doing exercises on the floor. It was Mr Klipspringer, who was living in the house as Gatsby's guest. Finally we came to Gatsby's own rooms, a bedroom, a bathroom and a study, where we sat down and drank a glass of some Chartreuse he took from a cupboard in the wall.

He hadn't once stopped looking at Daisy, and I think he gave a new value to everything in his house according to how much she liked it. Sometimes, too, he stared around his possessions in a confused way, as though in her presence none of it was any longer real. Once he nearly fell down some stairs.

His bedroom was the simplest room of all — except that on the dressing-table were a brush and comb set of pure, dull gold. Daisy took the brush with delight, and put it to her hair. Gatsby sat down and began to laugh.

"It's the funniest thing, old sport," he said. "I can't — When I try to — "

He had passed through two states and was entering upon a third. After his embarrassment and his joy he was filled with wonder at her presence. He had been full of the idea of her for so long — it was a dream which he had dreamed right through to the end. Now the waiting was over.

Recovering himself in a minute he opened for us two great cupboards which held his suits and ties, and his shirts, in several high piles.

"I've got a man in England who buys me clothes. He sends over what he has chosen at the beginning of each season."

He took out a pile of shirts and began throwing them, one by one, before us — shirts of fine cotton and thick silk, which covered the table in a confusion of many colours. While we admired them he brought more, and the soft rich pile rose higher. Suddenly Daisy bent her head into the shirts and began to cry wildly.

"They're such beautiful shirts," she cried. "It makes me sad because I've never seen such — such beautiful shirts before."

After the house, we were going to see the gardens and the swimming pool, and the sea-plane, and the midsummer flowers — but outside Gatsby's window it began to rain again, so we stood and looked at the misty surface of the Sound.

"If it wasn't for the mist we could see your home across the bay," said Gatsby. "You always have a green light that burns all night at the end of your sea wall."

He seemed to be thinking. Perhaps he realised that the immense importance of that light had now gone forever. When he had been separated from Daisy by a great distance, the light had seemed very near to her, almost touching her. It had seemed as close as a star to the moon. Now it was just a green light on a wall.

I began to walk about the room, examining various objects. A large photograph of an oldish man in sailing clothes attracted me.

"Who's this?"

"That? That's Mr Dan Cody, old sport. He's dead now. He used to be my best friend years ago."

"Come here quick!" cried Daisy at the window.

The rain was still falling, but in the west pink and gold clouds floated above the sea.

"Look at that," she whispered. "I'd like to get one of those pink clouds and put you in it and push you around."

I tried to go then, but they wouldn't let me.

"I know what we'll do," said Gatsby, "we'll have Klipspringer play the piano."

He went out of the room and came back with the young man, who looked embarrassed.

"I don't play well," he said. "I don't — hardly play at all. I'm out of practice — "

"We'll go downstairs," interrupted Gatsby.

In the music room Gatsby turned on a single lamp beside the piano. He lit Daisy's cigarette with a shaking hand, and sat down with her on a sofa in a dark corner of the room.

When Klipspringer had played "The Love Nest" he turned around unhappily.

"I'm all out of practice, you see, I told you I couldn't play. I'm all out of prac ——"

"Don't talk so much, old sport," ordered Gatsby. "Play!"

He played:

In the morning,
In the evening,
Ain't we got fun —

Outside the wind was loud. All the lights were going on in West Egg now. It was time for me to go home.

As I went over to say goodbye I saw an expression of uncertainty on Gatsby's face, as if he felt some doubt about his present happiness. Almost five years! All that time he had been building up his dream of her. How could any real person equal the immense power of the dream? There must have been moments that afternoon when Daisy had disappointed him.

As I watched him his expression changed. His hand took hold of hers, and when she said something low in his ear he turned towards her with a rush of feeling. Her voice had a magic that was beyond all dreams.

They had forgotten me, but Daisy looked up and held out her hand; Gatsby didn't know me now at all. I went out of the room and down the marble steps into the rain, leaving them there together.

6

Gatsby's Party

About this time a young reporter from a New York newspaper arrived one morning at Gatsby's door and asked him if he had anything to say.

"Anything to say about what?" inquired Gatsby politely.

"Why — any statement to give out."

It appeared that he had heard people talking about Gatsby, and thought there should be a story there for the newspapers. Gatsby's fame was growing, but it was the wrong kind of fame. All summer the hundreds of people who had attended his parties were spreading stories about his past — stories that were completely untrue.

I had reached the point of believing everything and nothing about him. It was not until much later that I learnt the truth about his beginnings, when he told me himself. But I am going to bring it in at this point in my story, to clear away all the false ideas.

He wasn't Jay Gatsby at all at first. His name was James Gatz, and he lived in North Dakota. His parents were poor and unsuccessful farm people — in his imagination he had never really accepted them as his parents at all. In his own mind he was a completely different person. Every night as he lay in bed he was troubled by strange thoughts, dreams of an extraordinary and beautiful world which was quite beyond his experience. But someone like James Gatz did not belong in such a world: he needed a new personality, and a new name. At the age of seventeen he invented Jay Gatsby, the kind of person he wanted to be. And to this idea of himself he was faithful until the end.

His new life began at the moment when he saw Dan Cody's boat on Lake Superior. For the last year James Gatz had been working his way along the south shore of Lake Superior, catching fish or digging in the sand for shellfish, or doing anything that would bring him food and a bed. He was still searching for something to do on the day that Dan Cody's boat sailed into Little Girl Bay. It was a beautiful boat. As he was wandering along the shore he looked up and saw it drop anchor in a dangerous area a little way from the shore. So he borrowed a rowboat, rowed out to the sailing boat and informed its owner that a wind might catch it and break it up in half an hour.

I suppose he smiled at Cody — he had probably discovered that people liked him when he smiled. And when Cody asked him his name, he had the answer ready: Jay Gatsby.

Cody was fifty years old then, and many times a millionaire, from his gold, silver and copper mines. He was still strong in body, but not in mind; and suspecting this, a number of women had chased him for his money, including Ella Kaye, the newspaper woman. He had been living on his boat, the *Tuomalee*, for five years, sailing along friendly shores, when he turned up in front of James Gatz.

To young Gatz, as he rowed out to the sailing boat, it represented all the beauty, charm and wealth in the world.

When Cody asked him a few questions he found that the boy was quick and highly ambitious, so he decided to employ him. A few days later he bought him a blue coat, six pairs of white trousers and a sailing cap. And when the *Tuomalee* left for the West Indies and the North African coast, Gatsby left too. He helped to sail the boat, acted as Cody's secretary, and sometimes even as his keeper. For when Dan Cody was drunk he was not responsible for his actions, and then he trusted in Gatsby to look after him. The arrangement lasted five years, during which the boat went three times around America. Then one night in Boston Ella Kaye came on board, and a week later Dan Cody died.

I remembered the photograph of him up in Gatsby's bedroom, a grey-looking man with a hard, empty face. He had been much too fond of women and drink — especially drink. That was the reason that Gatsby drank so little himself. Sometimes during his parties girls used to rub champagne into his hair; but apart from that he formed the habit of keeping away from alcohol.

And it was from Cody that he inherited money — twenty-five thousand dollars. But Gatsby never got the money: somehow, with the help of a clever lawyer, Ella Kaye managed to take all that remained of Cody's millions.

For several weeks after my tea party for Daisy I didn't see Gatsby. Mostly I was in New York, going around with Jordan and trying to make myself pleasant to her old aunt. But finally I went over to Gatsby's house one Sunday afternoon. I'd been there only two minutes when somebody brought Tom Buchanan in for a drink. I was surprised, of course, but the really surprising thing was that it hadn't happened before.

There were three of them, riding horses — Tom and a man named Sloane and a pretty woman who had been there before.

"I'm delighted to see you," said Gatsby, standing on his porch. "I'm delighted that you dropped in. Sit right down. Have a cigarette." He walked around the room quickly, ringing bells. "I'll get something to drink for you in just a minute."

Mr Sloane wanted nothing. A lemonade? No, thanks. A little

champagne? Nothing at all, thanks . . .

Gatsby turned to Tom.

"I believe we've met somewhere before, Mr Buchanan."

"Oh, yes," said Tom, polite, but obviously not remembering.

"About two weeks ago."

"Oh, that's right. You were with Nick."

"I know your wife," continued Gatsby, almost fiercely.

"That so?" Tom turned to me. "You live near here, Nick?"

"Next door."

"That so?"

Mr Sloane didn't enter into the conversation, and the woman said nothing either — until suddenly, after two cocktails, she became very friendly.

"We'll all come over to your next party, Mr Gatsby," she suggested. "What do you say?"

"Certainly; I'd be delighted to have you."

"That would be very nice," said Mr Sloane coldly. "Well — I think we ought to be going home." He got to his feet.

"Why don't you stay for supper?" said Gatsby, who wanted to see more of Tom.

"You come to supper with *me*," said the lady.

"Come along," said Mr Sloane — to her only.

Gatsby wanted to go with them, and didn't see that Mr Sloane didn't want him. "I haven't got a horse," he said. "I'll have to follow you in my car. Excuse me for just a minute."

The rest of us went out onto the porch, and Mr Sloane and the lady walked down the steps towards their horses.

"Where the devil did he meet Daisy?" said Tom angrily to me. "I don't like her running around by herself."

"Come on, Tom," Mr Sloane called. "We're late. We've got to go." And then to me: "Tell him we couldn't wait."

They all rode quickly down the drive. When Gatsby came out of the front door with his hat and coat, they had disappeared.

Tom was obviously worried at Daisy's going around alone,

for on the following Saturday night he came with her to Gatsby's party. Perhaps his presence there gave the evening its strange heaviness — it stands out in my memory from Gatsby's other parties that summer. There were the same people, the same immense quantities of champagne, the same noise and many-coloured activity, but I felt an unpleasantness in the air that hadn't been there before.

Tom and Daisy arrived as it was getting dark, and we walked over the lawn among the bright crowds.

"These things excite me *so*," Daisy whispered to me. "If you want to kiss me any time during the evening, Nick, just let me know and I'll be glad to arrange it for you."

"Look around," suggested Gatsby.

"I'm looking around. I'm having a wonderful —"

"You must see the faces of many people you've heard about."

Tom's scornful eyes looked over the crowd. "I was just thinking I don't know anyone here," he said.

"Perhaps you know that lady." Gatsby pointed to a splendid creature, looking more like a beautiful flower than a woman, who sat under a tree surrounded by admirers. Tom and Daisy stared, recognising a famous film-star.

"She's lovely," said Daisy.

"The man bending over her is her director."

He took them formally from group to group:

"Mrs Buchanan . . . and Mr Buchanan — the polo player."

"I've never met so many famous people," Daisy said. "I liked that man — what was his name? — with the sort of blue nose."

Gatsby told her his name and added that he was a film producer.

"If you don't mind, I'd rather not be called the polo player," said Tom.

Daisy and Gatsby danced. I was surprised by his graceful, old-fashioned way of dancing. Then we wandered over to my house and they sat on the steps for half an hour, while I remained watchfully in the garden.

We returned to the party, and as we were sitting down to supper Tom appeared. "Do you mind if I eat with some people over here?" he said.

"Go ahead," answered Daisy, "and if you want to take down any addresses here's my little gold pencil." She looked around after a moment and told me the girl with Tom was "ordinary but pretty". I knew then that except for the half-hour she'd been alone with Gatsby she wasn't having a good time.

The other people at our table were all rather drunk. Two weeks ago I had enjoyed these same people, but now their silly conversation annoyed me. It obviously offended Daisy. I could see that she disapproved of West Egg society.

I sat on the front steps with Daisy and Tom while they waited for their car.

"Who is this Gatsby anyhow?" demanded Tom suddenly. "Some big bootlegger?"

"Where did you hear that?" I inquired.

"I didn't hear it. I guessed it. A lot of these newly rich people are just big bootleggers, you know."

"Not Gatsby," I said shortly.

"Well, he must have had to work hard to get this odd collection of people together tonight."

"At least they are more interesting than the people we know," said Daisy.

"You didn't look so interested."

"Well, I was." Daisy began to sing with the music, in her warm, magic voice. "Lots of people come who haven't been invited," she said suddenly. "That girl hadn't been invited. They force their way in and he's too polite to send them away."

"I'd like to know who he is and what he does," insisted Tom. "And I'm going to find out."

"I can tell you right now," she said. "He owned some drugstores, a lot of drugstores. He built them up himself."

Their car came rolling up the drive at last.

"Goodnight, Nick," said Daisy.

I stayed late that night. Gatsby asked me to wait until he was free, and I waited in the garden until the usual swimming party had run up, cold but happy, from the black beach, until the lights went out in the guest rooms above. When he came down the steps at last his eyes were tired.

"She didn't like it," he said immediately.

"Of course she did."

"She didn't like it," he insisted. "She didn't have a good time."

He was silent, and I guessed at his despair.

"I feel far away from her," he said. "It's hard to make her understand."

He told me then what he wanted. He wanted her to go to Tom and say: "I never loved you." Then, after she was free, they would go back to Louisville and be married from her house — just as if it was five years ago.

"And she doesn't understand," he said. "She used to be able to understand. We'd sit for hours —"

"You shouldn't ask too much of her," I said. "You can't repeat the past."

"Can't repeat the past?" he cried unbelievingly. "Why of course you can!"

He looked around him wildly, as if the past were hiding here in the shadow of his house, just out of reach of his hand.

"I'm going to fix everything just the way it was before," he said firmly. "She'll see."

He talked a lot about the past, and I realised that he wanted to recover something, some idea of himself perhaps, that had gone into loving Daisy. His life had been confused and dis-ordered since then, but if he could only return to a certain starting place and go over it all slowly, he could find out what that thing was . . .

One autumn night, he said, five years before, they had been walking down the street when the leaves were falling, and they came to a place where there were no trees and the street was white with moonlight. They stopped here and turned toward each other.

His heart beat faster as Daisy's white face came up to his own. He knew that when he kissed this girl he would lose some of his own power. He would forever tie his dreams down to a human person — his grand imagination would no longer be free to wander through the universe. So he waited, listening for a moment longer to the music of the stars. Then he kissed her. At his lips' touch she became like a flower for him and the magic was complete.

7

A Hot Afternoon

It was when interest in Gatsby was at its highest that the lights in Gatsby's house failed to go on one Saturday night. The cars which turned into his drive, expecting a party, stayed for a minute and then drove sadly away. Wondering if he were sick I went over to find out.

The door was opened by an unfamiliar butler with an ugly face, who gave me a strange look.

"Is Mr Gatsby sick?"

"No." After a pause he added "sir" in an unwilling way.

"I hadn't seen him around, and I was rather worried. Tell him Mr Carraway came over."

"Who?" he demanded rudely.

"Carraway."

"Carraway. All right, I'll tell him." He shut the door.

My Finnish woman informed me that Gatsby had dismissed every servant in his house a week ago, and replaced them with half a dozen others, who never went into West Egg village, but ordered supplies over the telephone. The general opinion in the village was that the new people weren't servants at all.

Next day Gatsby called me on the phone.

"Going away?" I inquired.

"No, old sport."

"I hear you dismissed all your servants."

"I wanted somebody who wouldn't talk. Daisy comes over quite often — in the afternoons. These are people that Wolfshiem wanted to do something for. They're all brothers and sisters. They used to run a small hotel."

"I see."

He was calling up at Daisy's request — would I come to lunch at her house tomorrow? Miss Baker would be there. Half an hour later Daisy herself telephoned, and seemed relieved to find that I was coming. Something was up.

The next day was boiling hot, the hottest day of the summer. Gatsby drove me over to the Buchanans' house.

The sitting room was well-shaded against the sun, and it was dark and cool. Daisy and Jordan lay upon the big sofa.

"We can't move," they said together.

Jordan's fingers rested for a moment in mine.

"And Mr Thomas Buchanan, the polo player?" I inquired. Then I heard his voice in the hall, at the telephone.

Gatsby stood in the centre of the deep red carpet and stared around the room. Daisy watched him and laughed her sweet, exciting laugh.

"That must be Tom's girl on the phone," said Jordan.

We were silent. The voice in the hall rose high with annoyance: "Very well, then, I won't sell you the car at all . . . and don't trouble me about it at lunch time!"

"He's not really speaking into the telephone," said Daisy.

"Yes, he is," I told her. "It's a real deal. I happen to know about it."

Tom threw open the door and hurried into the room.

"Mr Gatsby!" He put out his wide, flat hand with well-hidden dislike. "I'm glad to see you, sir . . . Nick . . ."

"Make us a cold drink," cried Daisy.

As he left the room again she got up and went over to Gatsby and pulled his face towards her, kissing him on the mouth.

"You know I love you," she whispered.

"You forget there's a lady present," said Jordan.

At that moment a nurse came into the room, leading a little girl in a pretty white dress.

"My precious one!" cried Daisy. "Come to your mother!"

The child rushed across the room to the sofa and hid her face in her mother's skirt.

"The little precious! Stand up now and shake hands."

Gatsby and I leaned down and took the small unwilling hand. Afterward he kept looking at the child with surprise. I don't think he had ever really believed in it before.

"She doesn't look like her father," said Daisy. "She looks like me. She's got my hair and shape of the face." She bent her face down to the child's neck. "You little dream, you!"

Then she sat back upon the sofa.

"Goodbye, sweetheart!"

"Come, Pammy." The nurse took the child's hand and pulled her out of the room, unwilling but obedient.

Tom came back with our icy drinks. We drank thirstily.

"Come outside," he suggested to Gatsby, "I'd like you to have a look at the place."

I went with them out to the porch. The Sound was green and still in the heat. Gatsby pointed across the bay.

"I'm right across from you."

"So you are."

We had lunch in the dining room, darkened too against the heat. We talked with nervous brightness.

"What'll we do with ourselves this afternoon?" cried Daisy, "and the day after that, and the next thirty years?"

"Don't worry," said Jordan. "Life starts all over again when it turns cool in the fall."

"But it's so hot," insisted Daisy, almost in tears, "and everything's so confused. Let's all go to town!"

Tom was talking to Gatsby about his horses.

"Who wants to go to town?" demanded Daisy. Gatsby's eyes floated towards her. "Ah," she cried, "you look so cool."

Their eyes met, and they stared at each other, alone in space. With an effort she looked down at the table.

"You always look so cool," she repeated. It was a way of saying that she loved him, and Tom Buchanan saw. He was astonished. His mouth opened a little, and he looked at Gatsby, and then back at Daisy.

"You look like the man in that advertisement," she went on innocently. "You know the advertisement of the man —"

"All right," broke in Tom quickly, "I'm perfectly willing to go to town. Come on — we're all going to town."

He got up, his eyes still flashing between Gatsby and his wife. No one moved.

"Come on!" His temper was rising. "What's the matter, anyhow? If we're going to town, let's start."

"Are we just going to go?" Daisy objected. "Like this? Aren't we going to let anyone smoke a cigarette first?"

"Everybody smoked all through lunch."

"Have it your own way," she said. "Come on, Jordan."

They went upstairs to get ready while we three men went out on to the hot drive.

"Shall we take anything to drink?" called Daisy from an upper window.

"I'll get some whisky," answered Tom. He went inside.

Gatsby turned to me.

"I can't say anything in his house, old sport."

"She's got a voice which gives away her feelings," I remarked. "It's full of — " I hesitated.

"Her voice is full of money," he said suddenly.

That was it. It was the voice of a rich girl, a golden princess — that was its magic.

Tom came out of the house wrapping a bottle in a towel, followed by Daisy and Jordan.

"Shall we all go in my car?" suggested Gatsby.

"No, you take mine," said Tom, "and let me drive yours."

Gatsby did not like this idea.

"I don't think there's much gas," he objected.

"If it runs out I can stop at a drugstore," said Tom. "You can buy anything at a drugstore nowadays." He looked at Gatsby in a meaningful way.

A very strange expression passed over Gatsby's face.

"Come on, Daisy," said Tom, pulling her towards Gatsby's car. He opened the door, but she moved away.

"You take Nick and Jordan," she said. "We'll follow in your car."

She walked close to Gatsby, touching his coat. Jordan and Tom and I got into the front seat of Gatsby's car, and we drove off into the heat.

"Did you see that?" demanded Tom.

"See what?"

He looked at me sharply, realising that Jordan and I must have known all the time about Daisy and Gatsby.

"I've found out some things about this fellow" said Tom. "I've made an inquiry into his past."

"And you found he was an Oxford man," said Jordan.

"An Oxford man! Like hell he is! He wears a pink suit."

"Why did you invite him to lunch, then, if you feel like that about him?" demanded Jordan.

"Daisy invited him; she knew him before we were married — God knows where!"

We drove for a while in bad-tempered silence. Then as Doctor T.J. Eckleburg's eyes came into sight down the road, I remembered Gatsby's warning about gasoline.

"We've got enough to get us to town," said Tom.

"But there's a garage right here," objected Jordan.

With an impatient sound Tom stopped the car under Wilson's sign. After a moment the owner came out from inside and stared miserably at the car.

"Let's have some gas!" cried Tom roughly. "What do you think we stopped for — to admire the view?"

"I'm sick," said Wilson, not moving. "Been sick all day."

"Well, shall I help myself?" Tom demanded. "You sounded well enough on the phone."

With an effort Wilson left the support of the doorway and began to work the pump. In the sun his face was green.

"I didn't mean to interrupt your lunch," he said. "But I need money pretty bad, and I was wondering what you were going to do with your old car."

"How do you like this one?" asked Tom. "I just bought it."

"It's a nice yellow one," said Wilson. "But I could make some money on the other."

"What do you want money for, all of a sudden?"

"I've been here too long. I want to get away. My wife and I want to go West."

"Your *wife* does?" cried Tom.

"She's been talking about it for ten years. And now she's going whether she wants to or not. I just found out something funny is going on, and I'm going to get her away. That's why I been asking you about the car."

"What do I owe you?" demanded Tom roughly.

"One dollar twenty."

I realised that so far he didn't suspect Tom. He had discovered that Myrtle had some sort of life apart from him in another world, and the shock had made him ill.

"I'll let you have that car," said Tom. "Tomorrow."

Over the piles of ash, the giant eyes of Doctor T.J. Eckleburg were watching, but when I turned round I realised that other eyes were also looking at us. In one of the windows over the garage the curtains had been moved aside, and Myrtle Wilson was staring down at the car. Her eyes, wide with jealous terror, were fixed not on Tom, but on Jordan Baker, whom she thought to be his wife.

Tom drove on towards New York at high speed. The confusion in his simple mind was obvious. An hour earlier he had been sure of his wife and his mistress — and now they were both slipping rapidly out of his control. We caught up Gatsby and

Daisy, and argued about how we were going to spend the hot afternoon. Jordan wanted to go to a cinema; Daisy suggested that we hire five bathrooms and take cold baths. In the end, for no very good reason, we decided to hire a sitting room in the Plaza Hotel. We all said it was a mad idea — but at least it was a place where we could drink a mint julep.

The room was large and airless, and opening the windows only let in some hot air from the Park. Daisy went to the mirror to fix her hair.

"Open another window!" she said, without turning round.

"There aren't any more windows."

"Well, we'd better telephone for a hammer —— "

"Forget about the heat," said Tom impatiently. "You make it ten times worse by complaining about it."

"Why not let her alone, old sport?" remarked Gatsby.

There was a moment of silence.

"That's a great expression of yours," said Tom sharply.

"What is?"

"All this 'old sport' business. Where'd you get it from?"

"Now see here, Tom," said Daisy, "if you're going to make personal remarks I won't stay here a minute. Call up and order some ice and mint for the mint julep."

Tom took up the telephone and gave the order. Then, for some reason, he and I started talking about our college days. Suddenly, Tom turned to Gatsby.

"By the way, Mr Gatsby, I hear you're an Oxford man."

"Not exactly."

"Oh, yes, I understand you went to Oxford."

"Yes — I went there."

A pause. Then Tom's voice, scornful and unbelieving:

"I wonder when that could have been."

Another pause. A waiter came in with crushed mint and ice, and closed the door softly. We all looked at Gatsby. This important detail was to be cleared up at last.

"I told you I went there," he said.

"I heard you, but I'd like to know when."

"It was in 1919, I only stayed five months. That's why I can't really call myself an Oxford man. It was an opportunity they gave to some of the officers after the war."

I wanted to shout with joy. My faith in him returned.

Daisy smiled. "Open the whisky, Tom, and I'll make you a mint julep."

"Wait a minute. I want to ask Mr Gatsby one more question."

"Go on," Gatsby said politely.

"What kind of trouble are you trying to cause in my house anyhow?"

They were out in the open at last.

"He isn't causing trouble," said Daisy. "You're causing trouble, Tom. Please have a little self-control."

"Self-control! I suppose nowadays you're expected to sit back and let Mr Nobody from Nowhere make love to your wife!"

"I've got something to tell *you*," said Gatsby. "Your wife doesn't love you. She's never loved you. She loves me."

"You must be mad!" cried Tom.

Gatsby jumped up. "She only married you because I was poor and she was tired of waiting for me. It was a terrible mistake, but in her heart she never loved anyone but me!"

"Daisy!" said Tom. "What's been going on?"

"I told you," said Gatsby. "Going on for five years."

Tom turned to Daisy sharply.

"You've been seeing this fellow for five years?"

"Not seeing," said Gatsby. "No, we couldn't meet. But both of us loved each other all that time."

"That's a lie!" Tom burst out. "Daisy loved me when she married me and she loves me now. And I love Daisy too. Once in a while I go off on a little adventure, but I always come back, and in my heart I love her all the time."

"You're disgusting," said Daisy. She turned to me. "Do you know why we left Chicago? You didn't hear the story of *that* 'little adventure'?"

"Daisy, that doesn't matter now," said Gatsby. "Just tell him the truth — that you never loved him."

She looked at him blindly. "Why — how could I love him?"

"You never loved him."

She hesitated. "I never loved him," she said unwillingly.

"Not on our wedding trip?" demanded Tom.

"No."

"Not that day I carried you down the hill to keep your shoes dry? . . . Daisy?" There was tenderness in his voice.

"Please don't." Her hand was shaking as she tried to light a cigarette. Suddenly, she threw the cigarette and the burning match on the carpet.

"Oh, you want too much!" she cried to Gatsby. "I love you now — isn't that enough? I can't help what's past. I did love him once — but I loved you too."

"Even that's a lie," said Tom. "She never thought of you."

The words seemed to bite into Gatsby.

"I want to speak to Daisy alone," he said.

"Even alone I can't say I never loved Tom." Her voice was shaking. "It wouldn't be true."

"Of course it wouldn't," said Tom. "And from now on I'm going to take care of you, Daisy."

"You don't understand," said Gatsby. "You're not going to take care of her any more."

"I'm not?" Tom laughed. "Why's that?"

"Daisy's leaving you."

"Nonsense."

"I am, though," she said with an effort.

"She's not leaving me! Certainly not for a dishonest fellow like you! Who are you, anyhow? You hang around with Meyer Wolfshiem — I've been looking into your affairs."

"I won't stand this!" cried Daisy. "Oh, let's get out!"

"I found out what your 'drugstores' were." He turned to us. "He and this Wolfshiem bought up a lot of side-street drugstores here and in Chicago, and used them to sell alcohol. My friend Walter told me. But now they're concerned with something bigger — Walter's afraid to tell me about it."

I looked at Gatsby, and the expression on his face frightened me. It passed, and he began to talk excitedly to Daisy. But with every word she was drawing further and further into herself, so he gave up. Whatever courage she had had was definitely gone. She begged again to go.

"*Please* Tom! I can't stand this any more."

"You two go home, Daisy," said Tom. "In Mr Gatsby's car. Go on. He won't annoy you now — he realises it's over."

They went, without a word. After a moment Tom got up and began wrapping the unopened bottle of whisky in the towel.

"Want any of this? Jordan? . . . Nick?"

I didn't answer.

"Nick?"

"What?"

"Want any?"

"No . . . I just remembered that today's my birthday."

I was thirty.

It was seven o'clock when we got into the car with him and set off for Long Island.

Thirty — the promise of loneliness in front of me. A thinner list of unmarried friends, thinner hair . . . But there was Jordan beside me, who was wiser than Daisy. As we drove her pale face fell lazily against my shoulder.

So we drove on through the twilight towards death.

8

Accident

The main witness to the accident was the young Greek, Michaelis, who ran the café beside the ash piles. He told his story later, at the inquiry.

Some time after five he had wandered over to the garage and found George Wilson sick in his office — really sick, pale as his own pale hair and shaking all over. Michaelis advised him to go to bed, but he refused. Then they heard a violent noise upstairs.

"I've got my wife locked in up there," explained Wilson. "She's going to stay there till the day after tomorrow, and then we're going to move away."

Michaelis was astonished; they had been neighbours for four years, and Wilson did not seem the kind of man who had the force to do such a thing. So naturally Michaelis tried to find out what had happened. But Wilson wouldn't say a word — instead he began to question his visitor as if he suspected him, asking him what he'd been doing at certain times on certain days. He went back to his café.

When he came out again around seven he heard Mrs Wilson's voice, loud and angry, in the garage. A moment later she rushed out into the road, waving her hands and shouting.

The "death car" as the newspapers called it, didn't stop; it came out of the growing darkness, hesitated, and then disappeared around the next bend. The other car, the one going to New York, stopped a hundred metres further on, and its driver hurried back to where Myrtle Wilson lay in the road, her thick dark blood mixing with the dust.

We saw the cars and the crowd when we were still some

distance from the garage. "A crash!" said Tom. "We'll take a look." He stopped the car, and we got out. We saw the serious faces of the people at the garage door, and we could hear a strange groaning sound coming from inside.

"There's some bad trouble here," said Tom excitedly.

He stood on the tips of his toes and looked over a circle of heads into the garage. Then he made a rough sound in his throat and with a violent movement pushed his way through. Jordan and I followed when we were able to.

Myrtle Wilson's body lay on a work-table by the wall, and Tom was bending over it. Next to him stood a policeman, taking down names in a little book. The groaning sound was coming from Wilson, who was standing in the doorway of his office, swinging backwards and forwards and making his high, terrible call: "Oh, my God! Oh, my God! Oh, my God!"

Tom turned to the policeman.

"What happened? That's what I want to know."

"Car hit her. Killed at once. She ran out into the road. Driver didn't even stop his car."

"It was a yellow car," said a man. "Big yellow car."

Wilson seemed to hear this. "You don't have to tell me what kind of car it was. I know what kind of car it was!"

Tom walked over to Wilson and put his hands on his arms. "Listen. I just got here, from New York. I was bringing you my car. That yellow car I was driving this afternoon wasn't mine — do you hear?" He picked up Wilson, carried him into the office and set him down in a chair.

"Let's get out," he whispered to me, and we pushed our way through the crowd and out to the car.

As the car raced through the night I heard a low sound, and saw that the tears were flowing down Tom's face.

"The coward!" he said. "He didn't even stop his car."

Suddenly we were outside the Buchanans' house.

"Daisy's here," said Tom, looking up at two lighted windows. Then he turned to me. "I ought to have dropped you in West Egg, Nick. I'll telephone for a taxi to take you home. You and

Jordan can go into the kitchen and the servants will get you some supper — if you want any."

"No, thanks. But I'd be glad if you'd order the taxi."

Jordan put her hand on my arm. "Won't you come in, Nick? It's only half past nine."

"No, thanks." I was feeling a little sick and I wanted to be alone. I'd had enough of all of them for one day, and suddenly that included Jordan too. She must have seen something of this in my expression, for she turned sharply away and ran up the steps. I began walking down the drive.

A moment later I heard my name, and Gatsby stepped from between two bushes.

"What are you doing?" I inquired.

"Just standing here, old sport." After a minute he asked, "Did you see any trouble on the road?"

"Yes."

He hesitated. "Was she killed?"

"Yes."

"I thought so; I told Daisy I thought so. It's better that the shock should all come at once. She took it quite well." He spoke as if the effect of the accident on Daisy was the only thing that mattered.

"I got to West Egg by a side road," he went on, "and left the car in my garage. I don't think anybody saw us."

I felt so angry with him, I didn't tell him he was wrong.

"Who was the woman?" he inquired.

"Her name was Wilson. Her husband owns the garage. How ever did it happen?"

"Well, I tried to turn the wheel — " He broke off, and suddenly I guessed at the truth.

"Was Daisy driving?"

"Yes," he said after a moment. "But of course I'll say I was. You see, when we left New York she was very nervous, and she thought it would help her to drive. This woman rushed out at us just as we were passing a car coming the other way. It seemed to me that she wanted to speak to us — that she thought we were somebody she knew. Well, first Daisy turned away from the woman towards the other car, then she was afraid and turned back. I felt the shock as we hit her. I tried to make Daisy stop, but she couldn't.

"She'll be all right tomorrow," he went on. "I'm just going to wait here in case Tom tries to hurt her."

"He won't touch her. He's not thinking about *her*. How long are you going to wait?"

"All night, if necessary. Anyhow, till they go to bed."

I looked at the house; there were two or three lighted windows downstairs. "You wait here," I said. "I'll see if there's any sign of trouble."

I walked silently over the lawn to the kitchen window.

Daisy and Tom were sitting opposite each other at the kitchen table, with a plate of cold chicken between them, and two bottles of beer. Tom was talking, and from time to time Daisy moved her head in agreement. They weren't happy, and they hadn't touched the food and drink — and yet they weren't unhappy either. They looked as if they were planning something together.

As I went back to Gatsby I heard my taxi arriving.

"It's all quiet up there. Come home and get some sleep."

"No, I want to wait here till Daisy goes to bed. Good night, old sport." He turned to look eagerly at the house.

So I walked away and left him standing there in the moonlight — watching over nothing.

9

Murder

I hardly slept all night. Around four I heard a taxi go up Gatsby's drive, and at once I jumped out of bed and began to dress. I felt I had something to tell him, something to warn him about — and morning would be too late.

Crossing his lawn, I saw that his front door was still open. He was in the hall, leaning heavily on a table.

"Nothing happened," he said. "I waited, and at last she came to the window and stood there for a minute and then turned out the light."

He wanted a cigarette, and we began hunting through the great rooms for the cigarette box. That night his house seemed to me more enormous than ever — and strangely dusty, as if no one was living there. There were only two old cigarettes left in the box. We threw open the drawing-room windows and sat smoking out into the darkness.

"You ought to go away," I said. "They're sure to find your car."

"Go away *now*, old sport?"

He wouldn't consider it. He couldn't possibly leave Daisy until he knew what she was going to do. He was hanging on to some last hope that she might leave Tom, and I couldn't bear to tell him there was no longer any hope.

It was this night that he told me the strange story of his youth with Dan Cody. He told me because "Jay Gatsby" had broken up like glass against Tom's hardness, and didn't exist any more — the long game was over.

He wanted to talk about Daisy. She was the first "nice" girl he had ever known. He found her excitingly desirable. He went to her house, at first with other officers from the army camp, then alone. It astonished him — he had never been in such a beautiful house before. And because Daisy lived there, it had a feeling of mystery about it.

But he knew that he was in Daisy's house by accident. She knew nothing about him. He had let her believe that he was from the same sort of background as herself — that he was fully able to take care of her. He didn't tell her that he had no comfortable family standing behind him. He might have a splendid future as Jay Gatsby, but at present he was a penniless young man without a past. His soldier's uniform protected him, but when he lost that, he would be a nobody. So he made the most of his time. He took what he could get — and in the end he took Daisy, one quiet October night.

He had intended, probably, to take what he could and go — but now he found that he could not pull himself away from Daisy. He knew that Daisy was extraordinary, but he didn't realise just how extraordinary a "nice" girl could be. She disappeared that night into her rich house, into her rich, full life, leaving Gatsby — nothing. He felt married to her, that was all.

"I can't tell you how surprised I was to find out I loved her, old sport. I even hoped for a while that she would throw me over, but she didn't, because she was in love with me too. She thought I knew a lot because I knew different things from her. Well, there I was, going in quite the wrong direction to succeed in my plans for my life. I was getting deeper in love every minute, and all of a sudden I didn't care about my plans. What was the use of doing great things if I could have a better time telling her what I was going to do?"

On the last afternoon before he went abroad, he sat with Daisy in his arms for a long, silent time. It was a cold fall day, with a fire in the room. Now and then she moved and he changed his arm a little and once he kissed her dark shining hair. The afternoon had made them calm, as if to give them a deep memory for the long separation that was to come. They had never been closer in their month of love.

He did extraordinarily well in the war. He was made a captain even before he went to fight in France, and following the Argonne battles he was put in command of his unit. After the war was over he tried hard to get home, but for some reason he was sent to Oxford instead. He was worried now by Daisy's letters. She didn't see why he couldn't come. She wanted to see him and feel him beside her, to be sure that she was doing the right thing.

For Daisy was young, and she was feeling the pressure of the world around her, where her friends danced all night. She began to move again with the season; suddenly she was keeping half a dozen dates a day with half a dozen men. And all the time something inside her was crying for a decision. She wanted her life shaped now, immediately — and the decision must be made by some force that was close at hand.

That force took shape in the middle of spring with the arrival of Tom Buchanan. There was a solidness about his person and his position, and Daisy was relieved to put her future in his hands. The letter announcing her engagement reached Gatsby while he was still at Oxford.

It was getting light now on Long Island and we went about opening the rest of the windows downstairs.

"I don't think she ever loved him." Gatsby turned around from a window. "She was very excited this afternoon — she hardly knew what she was saying."

He sat down with a look of hopelessness.

"Of course, she might have loved him for just a minute, when they were first married — and loved me more even then, do you see?"

He had come back from France when Tom and Daisy were still on their wedding trip, and made a miserable journey to Louisville on the last of his army pay. He stayed there a week, walking the streets where they had walked together. When he left on the bus, he was penniless.

It was nine o'clock when we finished breakfast and went out

on the porch. The night had made a sharp difference to the weather, and there was a touch of autumn in the air. The gardener, the last one of Gatsby's former servants, came to the foot of the steps.

"I'm going to empty the pool today, Mr Gatsby. Leaves'll start falling soon, and there'll be trouble with the pipes."

"Don't do it today," Gatsby said. He turned to me. "You know, old sport, I've never used that pool all summer?"

I looked at my watch and stood up.

"Twelve minutes to my train."

I didn't want to go to the city. I didn't feel like work, but it was more than that — I didn't want to leave Gatsby. I missed that train, and then another, before I could get myself away.

"I'll call you up," I said finally. "About twelve."

"Do, old sport."

We walked slowly down the steps.

"I suppose Daisy'll call too." He looked at me anxiously.

"I suppose so."

"Well, goodbye."

We shook hands and I set off. Just before I reached my garden I remembered something and turned around.

"They're no good, any of them!" I shouted across the lawn, and I meant Tom and Daisy, and all Gatsby's fashionable "friends". "You're worth the whole lot of them!"

I've always been glad I said that. It was the only praise I ever gave him, because I disapproved of him from beginning to end. He raised his hand politely, then his face broke into that wonderful, understanding smile of his, as if the two of us were close together in a secret world.

"Goodbye," I called. "I enjoyed breakfast, Gatsby."

Up in the city, I tried for a while to write out a long list of figures, then I fell asleep in my chair. Around midday the phone woke me. It was Jordan Baker, who often called me up at this hour, because it was difficult for me to call her. Usually her voice came over the line as something fresh and cool, but today it seemed sharp and dry.

"I'm going down to Southampton this afternoon." She paused. "You weren't so nice to me last night."

This made me angry. "Last night, nothing mattered."

Silence for a moment. Then: "However, I want to see you."

"I want to see you, too."

"Suppose I don't go to Southampton, and meet you in town instead?"

"No, I don't think this afternoon."

"Very well."

"It's impossible this afternoon. Various — "

We talked like that for a while, and then suddenly we weren't talking any longer. I don't know which of us hung up, but I know I didn't care. I couldn't possibly have talked to her across a tea-table that afternoon.

I called Gatsby's house a few minutes later, but the line was busy. I tried four times; finally the operator told me the line was being kept open for a call from Detroit. Taking out my timetable, I drew a small circle around the 3.50 train. It was just twelve o'clock then.

Now I want to go back a little and tell what happened at the garage after we left. The story was told later at the inquiry by Michaelis, the owner of the coffee shop.

All night he had stayed with Wilson. Until long after midnight the garage was full of people. They left at last, and Michaelis was alone with Wilson, who was still swinging backwards and forwards and groaning. About three o'clock he grew quieter, and began to talk about his wife. He said that a couple of months ago she had come home from the city with her nose cut and bleeding.

"I thought then there was maybe something funny. And yesterday afternoon I found this." He opened a drawer in the desk and pulled out an expensive dog collar.

"I found this among her things. She tried to explain it, but I could see she was lying — I knew then she had some fellow." Wilson moved to the window and looked out. "I took her to the window and I said 'God knows what you've been doing, everything you've been doing. You may deceive me, but you can't deceive God — God sees everything!'"

Standing behind Wilson, Michaelis saw with a shock that he was looking at the eyes of Doctor T.J. Eckleburg, pale and enormous in the early morning light.

"That's an advertisement!" Michaelis told him.

"And then he killed her," said Wilson.

"Who did?"

"The man in the yellow car — her lover. She ran out to speak to him and he wouldn't stop. He *murdered* her. Well, I'm going to find out who that yellow car belongs to."

By six o'clock Wilson seemed quiet, and Michaelis went home to sleep. When he awoke four hours later and hurried back to the garage, Wilson was gone.

The police were later able to follow his movements as far as Gad's Hill. He was on foot all the time, and various people had seen a man on the road "acting sort of funny". He reached Gad's Hill about twelve o'clock, and bought a sandwich that he didn't eat. Then for two hours he disappeared from view. The police supposed that he spent that time going from garage to garage, inquiring for a yellow car. But no garage man who had seen him ever came forward. Perhaps he had an easier, surer way of finding out what he wanted to know? By half past two he was in West Egg, where he asked someone the way to Gatsby's house. So by that time he knew Gatsby's name.

At two o'clock Gatsby put on his bathing suit and told the butler that if anyone phoned he should bring word to him at the pool. He went to the garage for a water bed that had amused his guests during the summer, and the chauffeur helped him to pump it up. Then he gave orders that the open car wasn't to be taken out for any reason — and this was strange, because the front was damaged on the right side and needed repair.

Gatsby picked up the bed and set out for the pool.

No telephone message arrived, from Daisy or anyone else. The butler went without his sleep and waited for it until four o'clock — until long after there was anyone to give it to. I have an idea that Gatsby himself didn't believe it would come, and perhaps he no longer cared.

The chauffeur heard the shots — afterwards he only said that he hadn't thought anything much about them. No one went near the pool until I arrived from the station and rushed anxiously up the front steps. Then we hurried down to the pool, the chauffeur, butler, gardener and I.

There were small waves on the water, and the water bed with its load was moving down the pool. We could see a red line spreading from it through the water.

As we were carrying Gatsby's body towards the house the gardener saw the body of Wilson a little way off in the grass. The destruction was complete.

10

Saying Goodbye

Looking back I remember the rest of that day, and that night and the next day, only as an endless stream of police and photographers and newspapermen in and out of Gatsby's front door. I said as little as possible myself. A detective used the word "madman" as he bent over Wilson's body that afternoon; and the newspaper reports the next day took over this idea.

Later at the inquiry Michaelis's story showed that Wilson had suspected his wife of having an affair with another man. I thought then that the whole story might come out — but

Myrtle's sister Catherine, who might have said so much, didn't say a word. She swore that her sister had never seen Gatsby, that her sister had been completely happy with her husband, that her sister had been in no trouble at all. So, the decision reached by the inquiry was that Myrtle Wilson had been accidentally killed by a stranger; and George Wilson, driven mad by grief, had followed the track of this stranger, shot him and then shot himself. The case was closed.

But all this part of it didn't seem to matter. What mattered was that I found myself on Gatsby's side, and alone. From the moment I telephoned news of the murder, every question and every inquiry about him was addressed to me. At first I was surprised and confused; then, as he lay in his house and didn't move or breathe or speak, hour upon hour, it grew upon me that I was responsible, because no one else was interested.

I called up Daisy half an hour after we found him. But she and Tom had gone away early that afternoon.

"Left no address?"

"No."

"Any idea where they are? How I could reach them?"

"I don't know. Can't say."

I wanted to get somebody for him. I wanted to go into the room where he lay and promise him: "I'll get somebody for you, Gatsby. Don't worry. Just trust me."

I tried to telephone Meyer Wolfshiem, but he wasn't in. Then I went upstairs and looked quickly through the unlocked parts of his desk — he'd never told me definitely that his parents were dead. But there was nothing — only the picture of Dan Cody staring coldly down from the wall.

Next morning I sent the butler to New York with a letter to Wolfshiem, asking him to come out on the next train. I was sure he'd come anyway, when he saw the newspapers, just as I was sure there'd be a telegram from Daisy. But neither a telegram nor Mr Wolfshiem arrived. The butler brought back a letter from him. "This has been a terrible shock to me. But I cannot come down now as I am tied up in some very important business and cannot get mixed up in this thing."

When the phone rang that afternoon and the operator said there was a call from Chicago, I thought this would be Daisy at last. But it was a man's voice on the phone.

"This is Slagle speaking . . ."

"Yes?" I didn't know the name.

"Young Parke's in trouble. The police got him when he tried to sell those stolen bonds — they'd just got a message from New York giving them the numbers ——"

"Look here!" I interrupted. "This isn't Mr Gatsby. Mr Gatsby's dead."

There was a long silence, followed by a cry of fear, and the caller hung up suddenly.

I think it was on the third day that a telegram signed Henry C. Gatz arrived from a town in Minnesota. It said only that the sender was coming immediately.

He came. It was Gatsby's father, a solemn old man, in a tired, miserable state.

"I saw it in the Chicago newspaper," he said. "It was all in the newspaper. I started right away."

"I didn't know how to reach you."

His eyes moved about the room, seeing nothing.

"It was a madman," he said. "He must have been mad."

"Wouldn't you like some coffee?" I said.

"I don't want anything. Where have they got Jimmy?"

I took him into the room where his son lay, and left him there.

After a little while he came out, his mouth open, and a few tears on his face. He had reached an age where death no longer has the quality of terrible surprise; and when he looked around him now and saw the height and splendour of the hall and the great rooms opening out from it, his grief began to be mixed with pride. I helped him to a bedroom upstairs, and told him that all arrangements for the funeral had been put off until he came.

"I didn't know what you'd want, Mr Gatsby — "

"Gatz is my name."

" — Mr Gatz. I thought you might want to take the body back West."

He shook his head. "Jimmy always liked it better down East. He rose up to his position here. Were you a friend of his?"

"We were close friends."

"He had a big future before him, you know. If he'd lived, he would have been a great man. He'd have helped build up the country."

"That's true," I said, uncomfortably.

He lay down stiffly, and was immediately asleep.

That night I had a call from Klipspringer, the young man who had been Gatsby's house guest for so long. That would be another friend at Gatsby's grave.

"The funeral's tomorrow," I said. "Three o'clock, here at the house. I wish you'd tell anybody who'd be interested." I didn't want to put it in the newspapers and draw a sightseeing crowd, so I'd been calling up people myself. They were hard to find. "Of course, you'll be there yourself."

"Well, I don't think I . . . What I called up about was a pair of shoes I left there. Could you ask the butler to send them on? You see, they're tennis shoes, and I'm sort of helpless without them. My address is — "

I didn't hear his address, because I hung up in disgust.

The morning of the funeral I went up to New York to see Meyer Wolfshiem. He drew me into his office and offered me a cigar, remarking that it was a sad time for all of us.

"My memory goes back to when I first met him," he said. "He was looking for a job. A young officer just out of the army and covered over with decorations he got in the war. He was so poor he had to keep on wearing his uniform because he couldn't buy some ordinary clothes. He hadn't eaten anything for a couple of days. 'Come and have lunch with me,' I said. He ate more than four dollars' worth of food in half an hour."

"Did you start him in business?" I inquired.

"Start him! I made him. I raised him out of nothing. I saw

he was a gentlemanly-looking young man, and when he told me he was at Oxford I knew I could use him. He did some work for a friend of mine right away. We were like that," — he held up two fat fingers — "always together."

"Now he's dead," I said after a moment. "You were his closest friend, so you'll want to come to his funeral this afternoon."

"I can't do it — I can't get mixed up in it," he said. "When a man gets killed I never get mixed up in it."

I went home to West Egg, changed my clothes and went next door. It was raining. I found Mr Gatz walking up and down excitedly in the hall. His pride in his son and in his son's possessions was continually increasing.

"Had you seen your son lately?" I asked.

"He came out to see me two years ago, and bought me the house I live in now. He was always very generous with me."

A little before three the minister from the church arrived, and I began to look out of the windows for other cars. The servants came in and we all stood waiting in the hall. Mr Gatz spoke anxiously of the rain, and I asked the minister to wait for half an hour. But it wasn't any use. Nobody came.

After the funeral we drove to the graveyard, Mr Gatz and the minister and me in one car, the servants and the postman from West Egg in another. As we walked towards the grave I heard a car stop and then the sound of someone walking after us. I looked around. It was the man with the round glasses whom I had found wondering at Gatsby's books in the library during that first party.

I'd never seen him since then. I don't know how he knew about the funeral, or even his name.

"I couldn't get to the house," he said.

"Neither could anybody else."

"No! My God! They used to go there by the hundreds!" The rain poured down his thick glasses, and he took them off to watch Gatsby being lowered into the grave.

I tried to think about Gatsby then for a moment, but he was

already too far away. I could only remember, without anger, that
Daisy hadn't sent a message or a flower.

I see now that this has been a story of the West after all —
Tom and Gatsby, Daisy and Jordan and I, were all Westerners,
and perhaps we possessed some lack in common which made
us somehow unsuited to Eastern life.

After Gatsby's death the East was changed and spoilt for
me. So in October I decided to come back home.

There was one thing to be done before I left, because I
wanted to leave things in order. I saw Jordan Baker, and talked
over and around what had happened to us together, and
what had happened afterward to me. She lay quite still,
listening, in a big chair.

She was dressed to play golf, and I thought she looked like
a good fashion photograph. When I had finished she told me
that she was engaged to another man. I doubted that, though
there were several men who would have been eager to marry
her, but I pretended to be surprised.

"But you did throw me over," said Jordan. "You threw me over
on the telephone. I don't care a bit about you now, but it was a
new experience, and I felt a little odd for a while."

I got up to say goodbye. We shook hands.

"Oh, and do you remember," she added, "a conversation
we had once about driving a car? You said a bad driver was
only safe until she met another bad driver. Well, I met another
bad driver, didn't I? I made a wrong guess about you. I thought
you were rather an honest person."

Angry, and half in love with her, and enormously sorry, I
turned away.

One afternoon late in October I saw Tom Buchanan. He was
walking ahead of me along Fifth Avenue. Suddenly he saw
me and walked back, holding out his hand.

"What's the matter, Nick? Do you refuse to shake hands?"

"Yes. You know what I think of you. Tom," I inquired, "what

did you say to Wilson that afternoon?"

He stared at me without a word, and I knew I had guessed right about those missing hours. I started to turn away, but he seized my arm.

"I told him the truth," he said. "He came to the door while we were getting ready to leave. I told the butler to say we weren't in, but he tried to force his way upstairs. He was mad enough to kill me if I hadn't told him who owned the car. His hand was on a gun in his pocket —— " He broke off. "What if I did tell him? Gatsby deserved it. He ran over Myrtle like you'd run over a dog and never even stopped his car."

There was nothing I could say. I couldn't tell him that it wasn't Gatsby who had run over Myrtle, but Daisy.

"And I had my share of suffering — look here, when I went to give up that flat and saw that dog food sitting there, I sat down and cried like a baby. It was terrible ——"

I couldn't forgive him or like him, but I saw that what he had done was, to him, entirely right. It was all very careless and confused. They were careless people, Tom and Daisy — they broke up things and creatures, and left other people to deal with the confusion, while they returned to their money, or their carelessness, or whatever it was that kept them together.

I shook hands with him; it seemed silly not to, for I felt suddenly as though I were talking to a child.

Gatsby's house was still empty when I left — the grass on his lawn had grown as long as mine. I spent my Saturday nights in New York because those parties of his were with me so clearly that I could still hear the music and the laughter from his garden, and the cars going up and down his drive.

On the last night, with all my things packed and my car sold, I went over and looked at that huge house once more. On the white steps some boy had written a dirty word, which stood out clearly in the moonlight. I rubbed it out with my shoe. Then I wandered down to the beach and sat on the sand.

Most of the big houses along the shore were closed now, and

there were hardly any lights. As the moon rose higher the houses began to melt away, until gradually I became conscious of the old island here where the first Dutch sailors had landed — a fresh, green breast of the new world. The green trees that had made way for Gatsby's house had whispered once to those sailors on the shore; for a short magic moment they must have paused in wonder, face to face for the last time in history with a new world, the greatest of all human dreams.

And as I sat there thinking of the old, unknown world, I thought of Gatsby's wonder when he first picked out the green light at the end of Daisy's sea wall. He had come a long way to this blue lawn, and his dream must have seemed so close that he was sure to take hold of it. He did not know that it was already behind him, somewhere back in that immense darkness beyond the city, where the endless fields of the midwest rolled on under the night.

Gatsby believed in the green light, the magic promise of the future. He didn't realise that as we reach forward towards the dream, it moves ever further away from us. We press onward, like boats against the current, and all the time we are carried back into the past.

Questions

Questions on factual details

Chapter 1

1 Where was Nick's home town, and why did he want to leave it?

2 What was Nick's job in New York? Did he make enough money to live on?

3 What was Nick's connection with the Buchanans?

4 Who was Jordan Baker, and how did she know the Buchanans?

5 Who telephoned Tom during dinner? Did Daisy seem to know about Tom's relationship with this person?

Chapter 2

6 Who was Tom's mistress, and where did she live?

7 How did Nick meet her?

8 How did Myrtle Wilson and her guests spend the evening in her apartment?

9 What did Tom do to Myrtle at the end of the evening, and why did he do it?

Chapter 3

10 Give a short description of Gatsby's house and garden before one of his big parties.

11 How did Nick meet Gatsby?

12 What past experience did Nick and Gatsby have in common?

13 Why was Nick surprised to find that the man he was talking to was Gatsby?

14 What fault did Jordan have, and why didn't Nick blame her very much for it?

Chapter 4

15 What did Gatsby tell Nick about his family and education? Did Nick believe him?

16 What two things made Nick change his mind about the truth of Gatsby's story?

17 How do we know that Meyer Wolfshiem was involved with criminals and criminal activities?

18 Why was Daisy unhappy on the evening before her wedding? What did she mean when she said "Daisy's changed her mind"?

19 What happened to trouble Daisy's marriage?

20 What was Gatsby's request to Nick?

Chapter 5

21 Why do you think Nick refused Gatsby's business offer? How might it have changed his life?

22 Why did Gatsby want to go home during Nick's tea-party?

23 When Nick returned to the sitting room after standing under a tree, what change had taken place in Gatsby?

24 What things in Gatsby's bedroom suggested that he was in the habit of spending a great deal of money?

25 How had the meaning of the green light on Daisy's sea wall changed for Gatsby now?

Chapter 6

26 Why did James Gatz leave his parents' home, and give himself a new name?

27 Why did Gatz choose Dan Cody to introduce him to a new world?

28 What happened at the end of Tom's visit to Gatsby's house?

29 What were Daisy's feelings about the guests at Gatsby's party? How did Tom upset her?

30 "You shouldn't ask too much of her," said Nick to Gatsby. What was Gatsby asking Daisy to do?

Chapter 7

31   How did Tom find out that Daisy was in love with Gatsby?

32   Why did Tom take his own whisky to New York?

33   Why did Wilson want to take his wife away?

34   Myrtle Wilson saw Tom driving Gatsby's car. Do you think she knew that it wasn't his own car?

35   "I wanted to shout with joy." Why was Nick so pleased to hear Gatsby's explanation of how he went to Oxford?

36   At one point Daisy seemed ready to leave Tom. How did Tom manage to make her change her mind?

Chapter 8

37   Who drove Gatsby's car back from New York? Who had been in it on the drive from Long Island?

38   Why did Myrtle Wilson run into the road?

39   After the accident, what was Gatsby's main worry?

40   Why did Nick say that Gatsby was "watching over nothing"?

Chapter 9

41   Why did Gatsby refuse to go away and hide?

42   In what way did the young Gatsby deceive Daisy?

43   Why didn't Nick want to meet Jordan that day?

44   Why did Wilson murder Gatsby?

45   Where was Gatsby when Wilson shot him?

Chapter 10

46   What facts about Gatsby's murder were not discovered by the police?

47   What did Mr Gatz believe about his son's future? Why did Nick feel uncomfortable when he said "That's true"?

48   What was Nick trying to do in the days before the funeral. How successful was he?

49   When had Gatsby first met Meyer Wolfshiem? How had he helped Gatsby?

50   Why did Nick go to see Jordan before he went home?

Questions on the whole novel

1 What do Gatsby and the Buchanans have in common, and what is the main difference between them?

2 What is mysterious about Gatsby?

3 Imagine you are at one of his parties. Describe the scene.

4 Describe Tom Buchanan's appearance, and his character. Which of the following adjectives would describe him (Give examples from the book): strong-willed, violent, intelligent, sensitive, selfish, bad-tempered, cowardly?

5 What kind of personality has Gatsby built up for himself?

6 What part do motor cars and driving play in the story?

7 Give an account of Nick's tea party.

8 Describe Daisy's first visit to Gatsby's house. Why is it so important for him that she should see it?

9 How did Dan Cody change Gatsby's life?

10 What evidence do we have that Gatsby made some of his money in criminal ways?

11 Gatsby shows his love for Daisy in a number of extreme ways. Describe some of them.

12 How does the relationship between Nick and Gatsby change and develop during the story?

13 What part does George Wilson play in Gatsby's story?

14 "I am one of the few honest people that I have ever known," says Nick. How does this honesty affect his relationship with Jordan Baker?

15 Give examples of lack of honesty on the part of Jordan, Gatsby, Daisy and Tom.

16 Alcohol was forbidden, but a lot of drinking goes on in the book. What part does it play in the story?

17 Describe Gatsby's last day. How do Nick, Gatsby and Wilson spend the hours before the murder?

18 How are Daisy and Tom responsible for Gatsby's death?

19 How does Daisy fail Gatsby at the end, both before and after his death? What does this show about her character?

20 Give an account of the funeral, and the preparations for it.

Glossary

Note: words marked (Am.) are American uses.

acre a unit for measuring area; 1 acre = about 0.4 hectare

apartment (Am.) a flat

bay part of the sea enclosed in a curve of the land

bond (Am.) an insurance agreement

bootlegger someone who makes or sells alcoholic drink illegally

butler the chief male servant of a house

café a small restaurant where light meals and drinks are served

champagne an expensive white wine with a lot of bubbles

chauffeur a person employed to drive a car for someone else

check (Am.) a bill at a restaurant

cocktail a mixed alcoholic drink

divorce the official ending of a marriage

dozen a group of twelve

drive (n) a road that connects a private house with the street

drugstore (Am.) a pharmacy

elevator (Am.) an apparatus in a building for taking people to
different floors

embarrassed feeling anxious and uncomfortable, especially in a
social situation

engaged having agreed to marry

fall (Am.) autumn

furious very angry

gas/gasoline (Am.) petrol

golf a game in which people hit small white balls into holes in the
ground with special sticks

inherit to receive property from someone who has died

maid a female servant

marble a kind of white stone that is smooth, hard and cold to touch

millionaire a person who has a million dollars or pounds

mint julep an American drink in which alcohol and sugar are mixed,
poured over ice and to which mint is added

mistress a woman with whom a man has a sexual relationship which
is not socially acceptable

polo a game played between two teams on horseback who hit a ball on the ground with long-handled hammers

pony a small horse

porch a roofed entrance built out from a house

railroad (Am.) a railway

scandal a true or false story which brings shame to someone

scornful showing angry disrespect

sidewalk (Am.) the pavement

sofa a comfortable seat, wide enough for two or three people

telegram a message sent by electrical signals along wire

twilight the faint darkish light in the sky as day becomes night

water-ski a sport in which one travels over water on long narrow pieces of wood, being pulled by a boat

whisky a strong alcoholic drink made from grain